UNSPOKEN

MICHAEL ADANTE

First Printing, 2020

ISBN 978-0-6488279-0-0

Adante Media

6 Handcroft Street. Wavell Heights

Queensland, AUSTRALIA 4012

www.adantemedia.net

For Prat, Ruby & Scarlett.

TABLE OF CONTENTS

PROLOGUE

——— ◆ ◇ ◆ ———

The Majestic rode in the direction of fate. The tides that pulled it told a greater story, one that the crew on board was yet to see. A father and his two sons. Two brothers with auburn hair and sky lit eyes. Bonded together on a calm sea, the sky above clear and blazing. A great catch from the fisherman aboard as the sun glinted off the shimmering waves. The air and the mood onboard were light when Walter dove in. Casey watched his as his older brother disappeared into the deep blue, freckles scattered like constellations across his sun kissed nose.

It was quiet. The sound of silence stretched in time, as if to encompass what little light there was left to see. Scattered beams pierced through the blue water, the waves like crystals pulsing in rhythmic soliloquies.

Casey watched as his brother's body slowly sank. Watched as Walter tried to seize the very ocean itself. Yet, there was no hold for the young boy to grasp, the ocean proving to be a slippery grave.

Walter heard something like a muffled cry as he finally let his body sink, though the noise itself sounded light years away.

"Walter!" Casey screamed.

The words were lost to him, as finally his body surrendered. Like a feather he fell, calmly sinking into the dark grasp of the ocean depths. His arm still reached towards the light as if paused in a final reverie, his final moments captured in the silence surrounding him, and the contrasting beauty of the clear waters, shimmering in waves and sun. Just as the young boy's eyes began to flutter closed, a strange shadow broke the surface of the water above. But, the world was too distant now, he hardly registered it. There was an inviting gravity pulling him elsewhere, somewhere far, far away, and he let himself go.

Casey however, was not going to let his brother die that easily. He could just make out the shape of Walter's body. It was deep. Casey burst with his legs and arms forcing himself faster and faster, swimming with all the strength in his body. But, god, his brother just kept sinking. Casey's lungs were burning, he could feel the throbbing of his blood as he pushed himself even further. Kicking furiously and scooping the water with his palms.

It was a blink or an eternity but Casey reached him. At this point Casey's mind had long stopped thinking, something else had kicked in, his body acting on pure instinct. Walter's hand which was still reaching towards the surface, came into contact with Casey's, and Casey squeezed it tight pulling Walter towards him.

CHAPTER ONE

◆ ◇ ◆

A bus came to a halt, the sound of the breaks caught in the early afternoon, as the door opened, *csshh,* and eager passengers filed out, running into the arms of loved ones, some of which held up signs reading 'Welcome Home', others had inside jokes and colorful drawings, obviously designed by children.

Amidst all the love and reunion, a man who looked rather worse for wear, ducked his head to avoid hitting it as he exited the bus, a duffle bag thrown over his left shoulder. His face was stubbled with patches of grey which matched what was above, a slightly thinning hairline, and dark brown with streaks of grey. He made eye contact with a man who merely nodded and began walking towards his car.

The country side was a stark contrast to the passengers traveling through. A beautiful summer sun warmed the rolling hills, the glinting ocean waves crashed gently to their left. Just in the distance the small fishing town of Westport sat nestled in its bed. Casey's arm rested on the open window of his pickup truck. His brother Walter stared out in a similar fashion, but with an absence holding enough weight to steer anyone off course, one of the many reasons he wasn't driving.

Casey sat with a calm prideful air to him, his crisp polo shirt, neatly ironed, was the same color as the ocean foam. A sweet tie, blue and checkered was perfectly tied.

Walter on the other hand, in his ragged shirt and second hand tan jacket looked as if he were one step away from homelessness. The silence in the car was not that of ease, but of unspoken words and sentiments held hostage. As they turned around a long bend in the road the small fishing town of Westport came into view.

"The town looks different." Walter said, turning to look at his brother.

Casey kept his eyes steady on the road in front of him.

"It's not. It's the same as the last time you were here."

Walter's exhale was audible as he turned back towards his window. He let out a smirk.

Casey's eyes darted over and it became apparent as to why Walter had done so. A small fishing boat rang its bell as it prepared to dock, coming in from a night at sea. Walter traced it with his eyes as it slowly inched towards its place in the port, his heart tightened, sadness painted in his features.

"There's the Majestic…" Walter said.

Casey didn't reply.

From the tensing of his jaw and the way his grip hardened on the steering wheel, it was obvious this was a tender subject, and one not necessarily worth mentioning.

Despite the tension in the car, the world outside continued in its ways, the gulls circled above, and the town buzzed with life, people finishing an honest day's work. This almost made Casey smile. That was until he caught his brother's expression, haunted and lifeless. They couldn't have been more different. That's what their mom always used to say. Casey was the outgoing one, he won all the sports tournaments, even made it into the local paper. And Walter... Well... Most people never spoke about him.

~

The brothers woke up early the next morning, the doors to the pickup closing behind them as they set off into town. Casey, steady as always reached into a pocket in the door, fishing out his sunglasses. There was a slight glare, the morning sun rising in front of them. Walter was hardly present, his gaze distant and shaken, the brows on his forehead in constant furrow. Casey didn't bother asking if his brother was okay, he had seen Walter like this many times previously, it was nothing new. When horror becomes a daily occurrence, it ceases to become so for the parties' witness. Yet, through the eyes of the suffering it is but a constant agony. In likeness, Casey no longer had the capacity to hold space for Walter's condition, he had already spent half a lifetime wrapped in its coming and goings. And, when misery becomes normalized, compassion falls to ignorance.

They pulled up into the Westport memorial hospital at half past seven. A large industrial brick building with a scarce concrete parking lot. The truck came to a stop. Casey twisted the keys out of ignition and was out the door in a swift fluid movement, heading straight for the automatic double glass doors which served as entrance to the other what obtuse building. Meanwhile Walter struggled to even take off his seatbelt, and as he fumbled with the door handle it was evident that he needed help with even medial things such as this. Of-course the door was jammed. Casey stopped halfway to the hospital and turned around to see Walter amidst his struggle, the middle-aged man growing more and more frustrated with each attempt at failure. Casey muttered a curse under his breath before heading back to open the door from the outside.

"You need to fix that door." Muttered Walter, brushing past his brother and walking ahead.

Casey held in a retort, not now, this wasn't the time, this wasn't about him… He sighed, bottling up his annoyance and shut the passenger seat door, following after his brother. A brother whom Casey knew had no idea which direction to go.

Sure enough he was waiting for him at the entrance, staring up at the depressing pass for a hospital, frozen as if there were some invisible barrier preventing him from entering.

"Come on…" Casey muttered.

Walter didn't move for a good moment. Only when Casey began to look small in the distance of the long corridor before them, did Walter step over the threshold.

~

Room 307

Patient: June Treggar

Walter couldn't help but read the sign hanging on the door over and over again, not letting his mind think, not letting the racing pulse beneath his ribs be of any significance. Casey, however stepped right in. A snap of his finger broke Walter out of his loop and slowly, reluctantly he followed. His mother lay unconscious before him, the white of her skin hanging barely around brittle bones, it made her look one step away from death. She was practically a corpse… A shell of the mother he once knew. How had life passed by in a blink, how could it *still* be so… unbearable.

She had always told Walter it would get better, that he wouldn't be sick forever. Yet, here he was, at her deathbed, no better than he was twenty years ago.

A nurse was in the midst of checking June's vitals, she wrote something on her clipboard as the brothers entered. *Laura.* It read on her name tag. *Laura, Laura, Laura.* Walter just kept reading it, missed the smile she offered him as she quietly walked out, the only sound accompanying her was the squeak of rubber from her shoes gripping the polished floor, and the steady beep of his mother's vital monitor.

Walter watched Casey's legs as his brother sat himself at their mom's bedside, taking June's limp hand in his. Walter positioned himself as far away as possible, crossing his arms and leaning on the back wall, his eyes glued to the floor, which reflected a bright florescent light in its polished surface.

"Hey mom. Walter's here. He came just to see you."

Beep beep beep.

June was unresponsive.

Casey gestured his head towards the bed, "Say something Walt, let her know you're here."

Walter took a couple steps forward. "Hey mom. I'm here."

Casey motioned with his hand, telling Walter to come closer. Walter didn't move and instead only raised his voice.

"I'm here!"

He practically shouted the words, and they bounced uncomfortably off the thin walls of the hospital room. Casey sighed, June of course still offered nothing to show that she was able to hear them.

"What's wrong with you Walt… This is your mom. Your *mom*." Casey shook his head. "The last thing she asked for was to see you."

"I…" The words wouldn't come out of Walter's mouth, his face was pale and honestly looked like he was about to be sick. "Maybe… Maybe she's already… passed on."

This set something off in Casey as he glared sharply towards his brother.

"Really Walt?" Casey clenched his jaw and took his eyes away from Walter. "Just wait for me outside."

"I'm sorry, I didn't mean… for it to sound that way…"

Walter shuffled uncomfortably in his place, his hands twining in one another nervously. Casey continued to avoid Walter's eyes gently stroking his mother's hand, and left Walter to the silence, which held more weight than any words.

"I'll just be outside then." Walter mumbled, as he shuffled out into the hallway.

He shoved his hands into his pocket and leaned against the wall beside June's door. Frustrated at his own incompetence, Walter festered in his own thoughts, letting them spin self-deprecating stories, in turn resigning himself to the isolation which had kept him *protected* for as long as he could remember.

The daily goings of the hospital ran like an organized machine. Nurses and doctors making regularly timed checkups on patients, ticking and noting things on identical clipboards. There was a flurry of noise around him: the low buzzing of fluorescent lights, murmuring family members coming to visit their loved ones, the ring of phones and the wild orchestra of beeping machines. Walter tried not to hear it all, but it was impossible to ignore, it was all so loud when stacked together, too many voices, too many sounds. Walter winced as they soon threatened to overwhelm him. In some attempt for comfort his eyes darted over to a clock on the far wall, how long was he meant to wait here.

It had only been two minutes.

Tick… Tick… Tick…

Like hypnosis the steady rhythm of the clock drowned out the hospital sounds, it became Walters only object of focus, the only real thing around him. *Ahh.* His mind seemed to say, relief. It captivated him, and his eyes attuned to the second hand flicking forward. So precise, so reliable.

"Walter." The voice was distant, muffled and barely audible.

"Walter!" Still no reaction.

"Hey!" Casey began clicking his fingers in front his brothers face, trying to snap him back into this world.

Walter suddenly came to, shaking his head as if coming out of a dream. The sounds of the hospital rushed in like a dammed river and there was Casey standing in front of him. *When had he gotten there.*

"Let's go." Casey said, walking off without a moment's hesitation.

Walter followed like an obedient dog, still caught in a daze. "You're worse than I thought." Casey mumbled, but Walter didn't hear it, not over the drowning of the hospital choir. They rounded a corner and approached the nurse's station a couple meters ahead, where June's nurse was scribbling illegible words on their mother's medical chart. She looked up before they reached and her lips drew themselves into a thin line.

Not letting that deter him, Casey walked straight up to her, bypassing any formalities and getting straight to the point. "How is she doing?"

The nurse scanned her eyes up and down the chart as if she were reading it for the first time. The sad truth was that she knew exactly how June was doing, she just wasn't ready to meet Casey's eyes when she relayed the news. Laura cleared her throat, steeling herself, and preparing her professional answer.

"She's stable, no strange anomalies. But, as you can see she's still unconscious, and there is no saying when she will wake up next." Laura managed to look up from her clipboard and offered the brothers a gentle smile. "But, she's stable."

The glimmer of hope that Laura offered allowed Casey to smile back. He wanted so badly to hear his mother speak again, to see even a blink from her weary eyes. If it wasn't for the kindness and understanding way Laura spoke, Casey may have set off on a rant about how the hospital wasn't doing enough, how they should be doing more to make sure his mom was healthy. But, Casey let the frustration fizzle out, acknowledging that he only wanted someone to release his emotions on, a scapegoat, and the fact that Walter was here, and acting… Well, the way he acted, didn't help.

"Could you please make sure someone calls me if she wakes… Or you know… If something happens." Casey spoke, trying to find optimism in his words, but the only smile that arose was forced.

"Of-course." Laura replied, giving a little nod and meeting Casey's smile with a genuine one of her own.

The brothers walked off together in silence.

~

It was a slow, lazy Sunday. Families milled about at their own leisure, walking through the town centre, idling from shop to shop, children running ahead of their parents, skipping and playing through the streets.

Westport was a safe town, one where parents felt comfortable letting their kids bike to friends' houses unleashed and unrestrained. Here, everyone knew each other, and all the familiar faces were out and about as the sea breeze blew in fresh against the cloudless sky.

The two brothers had just parked in the centre parking lot, and they followed the thin flow of people down a wide sidewalk. Even through the tense silence, there was a love between them. It mostly went unspoken, for neither knew how to express what they felt, they never had any practice. It can be hard sometimes for a man to say what's on his mind, especially to another man, especially in a world where emotions are reserved for women, and the neutral face a man holds is his reserve of manhood. Or so that's what the brothers were brought up to believe.

Casey finally broke the silence with the only thing that came to his mind.

"How's the weather in the city?"

"Same as here." Walter replied. "We get *your* weather two days later."

Casey nodded repeatedly, an interested furrow of his brow to indicate he was listening. He was trying, that much could be said. But, as usual, words fell short and they continued heading down the sidewalk in that all too familiar silence. At least the bright sound of children laughing and families going about their day distracted from their absent words. Casey was about to speak again, when someone caught his eye.

Julia.

His heart seized for a moment, lurched from its sinking place, and for just a moment soared with the seagulls above. She was gorgeous. Dark chestnut hair fell in natural waves, and she carried an air about her that made anyone feel welcome. Casey couldn't help but smile as he watched her wave to a friend across the street. Anyone who met Julia could tell she had a good childhood, one spent running through forests and swimming in the ocean. She had a calm to her that only arises from many years spent in nature, unlike those who moved here from the city. He watched as she walked arm in arm with her husband. Slowly the smile faded from Casey's lips. Patrick was there as well, their teenage son. He was well known around town for getting himself into trouble. It was only last week that Fearson, the local shopkeeper caught Patrick stealing a six pack of beer.

Luckily for him, the town was so intimate with one another that Fearson let the boy off with a warning. Although he probably would have avoided the trouble regardless, considering that Patrick's old man was Officer John Griffin. He'd joined the force straight out of high school, following in his father's footsteps.

Casey observed as the family meandered into the local diner, one his old classmate Shirley had recently taken over from her parents. Slyly, Casey glanced over at his brother. Walter was in his own world as usual, taking in all the familiar surroundings as if he was a tourist.

"You hungry Walt?"

His brother shrugged. "Yeah I guess."

Casey nodded. "Yeah me too."

The bell hanging over the diner door rang as they entered. Casey gestured with his head to a table by the far window and Walter followed behind quietly. It took a moment's survey to find who he was looking for, and he positioned himself tactfully on the right side of the window booth to make sure their view was unobstructed. Walter sat down with a slump opposite him, immediately burying a cheek in his palm and staring out the window at the passing people. There were menus already waiting for them on the table. Casey pushed one over to Walter, pulling him out of his distant daze. Casey knew how much of a chore it was to get any decision out of Walter, so better to get him thinking about it now rather than later.

Casey however, already knew what he wanted, and it wasn't on the menu. He fixed his gaze on Julia who sat facing him a few booths down. She hadn't noticed that he had walked in and was caught-up in the conversation around her. Patrick sat sulking beside her, the peak of his teenage years obviously taking their toll on his mood. He had been a good kid when he was younger, Casey always remembered him as a bright-eyed imaginative boy. It was crazy how much someone could change once adolescence came around. He had seen it first hand with Walter as well. It was a tough time for a lot of people, a time where some never managed to grow out of.

"They have a sandwich called *The Majestic*"

Walter's voice snapped Casey's attention away and back to their table.

"Just pick something." He replied, ignoring the tone in which Walter spoke.

"What are you getting?"

"I'll eat later."

The oddities of Casey's behavior went unnoticed by Walter, he was too wrapped in his own world to pick up on the little things, such as the nervous way Casey's knee bounced, or the distant gaze that went way beyond their booth.

An old weary woman approached their table. Walter noticed her from the corner of his eyes but kept himself fixed on scanning the menu. She stood there for a moment in silence before taking out her small waitress note pad.

"Can I get you boys anything?" The sentence came out like a sigh. She was obviously resigned to her job and that mood fell off her shoulders like heavy boredom.

Casey managed to pull up a smile, from no place of joy mind you, rather one of formality. Whilst Walter took his time to look up from the menu, every passing second leaving Casey more and more agitated.

Finally, as he turned to her, her name tag *Helen* caught his gaze and held it, before he asked, "Helen, this number eleven. *The Majestic*, does it come with salad?"

"Yes." She sighed. "Salad and fries."

Walter nodded in interest.

"And Helen, why is it called *The Majestic?*" Walter inquired further.

"Walter!" Casey's voice came out muted yet, forceful. Which was followed by a pressing glare. "Just give him the sandwich with coffee." she scribbled down the single order. "On wholegrain." She nodded. "Thanks, *Walter.*"

She took the menu from him and Casey offered her that same formal smile. Helen left without so much as a whisper. As soon as she turned her back, Casey's smile fell off his face and was replaced with a disapproving frustration. He shook his head in Walter's direction.

"What?" Walter pried.

Casey ignored him, shoving the frustration down and looked away from his brother.

There she was.

Julia looked concerned. And sure enough, Patrick was acting up again. It pulled on Casey's heart to see her that way.

"I was just asking…" Walter's voice mumbled from the sidelines.

The frustration rose through Casey's nostrils. He curried his face in his palms for a split second before he snapped.

"Why?! Why were you asking?! Many fishermen have sailed the damn Majestic and many have died. Life isn't one big story about *you!*"

The words hit Walter in punches and the pain was evident in his features. He turned away towards the window.

"Maybe you're right Walt." Casey continued. "Maybe that *is* dad's sandwich. Or rather he's garnish that floats outside."

Walter's voice dropped low. "Don't talk about dad that way."

Casey scoffed. "You haven't changed one-bit, Walt."

Walter didn't let his gaze leave Casey's.

"Why did you even call me down here." Walter jabbed.

"I told you. Mom asked for you." Casey sighed. "Said she wanted to see you. Tell you something."

"What?"

"I don't know. You'll have to wait for her to tell you herself."

"What is it?" Walter said through clenched teeth.

"I said she'll tell you herself."

"It's important isn't it? Tell me!"

"Alright! Fine! You want to know? I'll tell you." There was a slight pause. "You're adopted, Walt. That's it. That's moms big secret."

For a moment Walter didn't believe him, but then it began to sink in. He had always felt like an outcast, had always been so distant, he felt like an alien within his own family. This must be the reason why. Walter was speechless. He slumped back in his chair with a weary resignation.

"Walter…" Casey said. His brother didn't respond. "You're not adopted, man. I was joking. I told you, I don't know what it is, honestly. She'll tell you when she wakes up."

Walter felt the fool once more. How had he let himself believe that? Perhaps he wanted a reason, a diagnosis to explain why he felt so misplaced. Anything to take the fault off his own shoulders. It would be so much easier to throw the blame on someone else.

And in some unconscious act of deflection Walter replied, "If she wakes."

"Mom's going to be fine."

Casey genuinely looked optimistic which brought a wave of comfort over Walt. The brothers exchanged a yielding nod to one another. For now, the tension had eased, as was so natural with them. Never a steady day of feelings, always a ride of tension and nerves, with moments of calm waters. And, at the root of it all was an undying love. One that only brothers can share, brothers who for at least a small portion of their lives, knew what it meant to truly be there for one another.

Walter returned his attention to the people filtering by outside his window, whilst Casey looked back over towards Julia. This time her eyes were waiting for him. John's back was facing Casey, but it was obvious from how Julia's attention switched back and forth between him and Casey, who her focus was on. She continued to listen to John, nodding when appropriate, but when she could, she let her eyes return to Casey. And when she did, the world stopped. It was as if her heart flew between zero gravity, threatening to send her floating forever into eternal space.

The same went for Casey, he couldn't help feel the esoteric pull, the one that goes beyond all reason, one worth sacrificing everything for.

This kind of love works in polarity, whilst every glance from her made him whole, it equally tore him apart, threatening to undo him.

Julia made a good show of replying to John, she even laughed at his jokes, but nothing of what she gave to Casey in her brief glances was reciprocated to her husband. Casey held her heart and she his. Enough so that even as he watched her laughing with another man it softened him, made him smile to see her happy.

Casey didn't even realize that his lips were turned up, and that his eyes burned with love, until Walter spoke.

"What's so funny?"

Casey quickly brought his eyes back to Walter. Even his brothers lifeless face couldn't dampen his mood.

"It's just, you know… Us. Here. After all that's happened." Casey noticed the waitress approaching with Walters food, and smiled again. He gestured towards her with his eyes. "Eat up."

The sandwich looked delicious, a layer of chicken and bacon, with fresh green lettuce and a drizzling sauce oozed out the side of well-made ciabatta. The coffee was steaming inviting swirls into the air. Walter felt himself salivate, he was hungrier than he thought. When the food arrived before him, he couldn't help but get excited. The mingling smells eased their way into his nostrils and he set to removing the toothpick which held the sandwich together.

With Walter distracted Casey looked back over towards Julia, and when she met his gaze he motioned towards the bathroom. She winked at him discretely, acknowledging what he intended. "Stay here, Walt I'm going to use the restroom."

Walter didn't even reply as he sunk his teeth into a juicy bite of chicken, the bacon on top tickling the tip of his palette. He made a soft mumbling moan, obviously appreciating the cooking. Casey got up and signaled over to the waitress to bring one more, pointing to their booth. She acknowledged him with a little nod and headed over to the kitchen.

John was rambling on like always about some new tech toy that his friend Andrew just bought, and Julia listened enthusiastically as he spoke about it with passion. He paused for a moment to take a sip of his soda and she took the opportunity to excuse herself.

"Excuse me darling. Washroom calls."

He nodded to her mid-sip and she gracefully slipped out of the booth.

The restaurant was busy, the sound of clinking plates and conversation a nice texture in the air, happy families enjoyed their Sunday lunch and Walter in this moment, felt something like ease. He let himself enjoy where he was, eagerly stuffing his face.

With Julia's absence however, a heavy silence fell over John and Patrick. They sat across from each other staring in opposite directions. It was as if they were strangers to each other, strangers forced to live in the same house, forced to spend time together, forced to like one another. They were at a stage when the bond between father and son gets put to the test, the young maturing male pushing against his father's authority and his power, no longer a child, but still too young to possess his own freedom. An unspoken feud, a bitter war of dominance wages. One can only hope that the inevitable schism isn't large enough to permanently sever what was once a bond of love.

~

Walter saved a full bite for himself, and it lay waiting on his plate as he calmly sipped on his americano coffee. Casey's food arrived a good while ago, and the steam off his sandwich had long since dissipated, the bread turning soft and moist from the juices sitting.

"Hah! You think that's funny!?" Patrick's voice rose above the diners ambience, slamming against the boundaries of the building.

Everyone in the restaurant stopped mid bit or conversation to follow the disruption.

"Keep your voice down." John hissed through a clenched jaw.

Patrick slammed his fist on the table, and its echo shook the room. He practically spit on his father with his glare and burst away from the table. Then, mid stride, the teenager hurled his half-eaten sandwich like a fastball, landing it perfectly square on his father's melon-like face. A wicked smile of victory spread over Patrick's face. He flung open the door so forcefully that the bell above clanged spastically, and the restaurant was left in an eerie silence. Only the sounds of the kitchen and the cheesy diner seventies music sounded.

John was fuming, lettuce, tomatoes and sandwich grease slipped down his face.

"Yeah, you better leave jackass! And don't even think of coming home tonight, spoilt rat!"

The officer wiped his face and threw the napkin down forcefully towards the door.

Walter was unamused as he watched, casually sipping on his coffee. He had seen much worse in the many mental facilities he had been too.

The diner began to recover from the drama, people returned to their conversations and the waitresses shook their heads in disapproval, Casey finally emerged from the bathroom. He looked more tired than when he went in, his hair disheveled and tie loose around an undone top button.

"What the hell were you doing in there? You took ages." Walter asked, frowning.

Casey just dug into his sandwich, taking a huge bite and savoring its flavor.

"I thought you weren't hungry." Walter commented.

"I am now."

Walter continued to examine his brother with suspicion. Meanwhile, Julia, elegant as ever, strode out of the bathroom, her hair, just like Casey's was slightly out of place. She adjusted it with her hands as she made her way back towards John.

"Where's Patrick?" Julia inquired as she slipped into her seat.

Casey watched her from his place, amidst the bites of sandwich. Her eyes never returned to his. That was all he was going to get. She had a family, and he was just the man on the side, the garnish outside he had joked about. Casey slumped deeper into his seat, the sandwich became a grey distraction from the sinking feeling in his chest. His eyes dulled as he watched John animatedly recount the events leading up to Patrick's outburst. Julia posture was poised as ever, her eyes focused on John. The words that came out of her mouth were too soft for Casey to hear, but he could tell from John's reaction that she was putting him in his place. If ever there was a time to leave, it was now. But, Casey couldn't find the motivation to pull himself up.

His coffee was lukewarm, and he could hardly taste it over the swirls of emotions and feeling inside. Walter had noted a couple things since Casey's return but he remained silent, staring like always out the window. There is no weight similar to watching someone you love with another person. The strings that pull at our hearts yearn for warmth, yearn for that particular love, yet find no earth in which to ground it. In moments such as these the mind tends to dissociate itself from the world, uses any thought or memory, or distracting story to soar over what we really feel inside. It takes true bravery to face the church bells, which for some cruel reason strike backwards, leaving us dissonant and empty, as Casey felt at that moment.

CHAPTER TWO

◆ ◇ ◆

The night sky was clear like silk, a warm blanket over the Treggar family house. Casey and Walter sat facing out towards the calm blue ocean, reclining on the back deck whilst the moon shone full and reflected cleanly in the waters below.

Casey sighed.

"Still nothing."

He hung up the phone and took a long heavy pull from his cigarette. Walter felt his brother's thoughts adrift with worry. There had been no update from the hospital on their mother's condition. They both looked out onto the port, the sound of boats against the docks and wind through ropes and sails, filtered through the air and landed on their deck.

Walter flicked the ash off his cigarette and in a meagre attempt, tried to take Casey's mind off their mom.

"I heard you got some sorta promotion." He offered.

"Yeah." Casey dragged on his cigarette. "Trainee foreman."

Walter nodded his head with an enthusiastically impressed expression.

"Nice job."

"Thanks."

Casey didn't seem anywhere near as enthused, as if the promotion meant nothing. His eyes were lifeless, windows into nothingness.

"Who did you hear that from?" Casey asked.

"Mom. Who else."

"Was that the last time you spoke to her?"

Walter nodded.

They sat in silence for a moment.

"How did she get sick?" Walter whispered, turning to look at Casey.

Casey sighed and pulled on his cigarette, it was nearing the end.

"She'd been acting different for a couple weeks, like she was lost in a haze. Always dazed and slightly unsure of herself. They think something must have fallen on her, maybe when she was putting away groceries or moving dad's old stuff."

Casey flicked his cigarette butt off the back porch as an uncomfortable silence settled.

"It's a fucking stroke isn't it?" Walter replied after the quiet became too unbearable.

"You know it is."

Walter took one last drag. "Maybe you should call again."

"They'll tell us when something happens."

Walter didn't reply, staring off into the distant horizon that glowed silver in light of the fully waxed moon.

"Why do you smoke out here?" He asked.

"I don't want the house to smell like a fucking ash tray." Casey replied.

"Why? It's not like mom's going to tell you off."

Casey gave his brother a slightly annoyed glare.

"I just want to keep the house as it is. It still smells the same as when we were kids. Mom didn't even let dad smoke inside."

"She didn't, did she?"

Walter managed a light hearted scoff. Casey smiled back.

"He was a stubborn old seahorse, got his way with almost everything. But, she was the boss when it came to this house. I could hear him from my window moaning like a spoilt kid as he puffed out here. Didn't matter if it was his birthday, raining, or even after they'd done it."

Walter chuckled.

"Poor guy. He gets laid one minute, the next he's freezing his nuts off in the cold. I'm surprised he never bought a gas heater for the porch."

"He was too cheap for that." Casey chimed. "This was moms house, we just happened to live here."

Walter looked around the roof, like a perspective buyer, "It's weathered some hard days. But... nothing stands forever."

Casey nodded, waiting for Walter to go on, but his brother said nothing more, lost once again in some distant reverie. As if in response to what lay ahead, the currents in the ocean picked up, slapping turbulent waves against the docked boats.

~

The next morning the two brothers rode through the richer part of town. Large colonial houses with pillars out-front lined the streets. Casey was somewhat fidgety as his eyes darted between the dash clock and traffic.

"I'm just going to drop you off, okay? Time's tight."

"Why can't I stay with you?" Walter replied, his arms folded.

Casey could tell Walter wasn't in the best mood, nor did he want to be dropped-off like a kindergartener at day care.

"I can't watch you every second, Walt. I have work and things to do, plus I wouldn't know what to do, when… you know."

"You don't have to do anything. I'm fine."

Casey gave his brother a doubtful look from the side of his eyes.

"It's only for a couple weeks. You can go home when…" Casey's words froze mid-sentence. "You know when."

Walter's response was bitter.

"Mmm. Great. I can't wait to go back there."

Casey shook his head as he concentrated on the road ahead.

"Come on Casey, trust me, please."

Casey didn't respond, they had almost arrived. He could practically feel Walter's resignation as they pulled up into the local group home.

"Cheer up Walt, you might remember this place."

"Jesus. What the hell, Case? It's our old school… I'm not living in our fucking school."

This was just another slap in the face for Walter, he wasn't a child that needed taking care of. He wasn't so hopeless that he couldn't be left alone. Why couldn't Casey have more faith in him? Casey only smiled lightly.

"Oh god not her…" Walter grumbled.

Heather Mazzanno waited at the front door with her arms folded like a Victorian era principle. She was a dump truck of a woman, one would think she were nearing her seventies, but she had just had her fifty-fifth birthday last week.

"What are you talking about, you love Ms. Mazzanno." Casey jeered.

Walter glared fiercely at his brother.

Casey laughed at Walter's reaction, giving him a brotherly pat on the shoulders.

"You have my number. Call me if you need anything."

"Yeah, fine…" Walter mumbled.

"I'll come pick you up as soon as I can. We'll go pay mom a visit then grab a bite."

Casey leaned over the seat to give his brother a hug but Walter remained facing forward with his arms crossed.

Casey sighed. "Look after yourself, Walt."

Walter left the car in somewhat of a huff, not bothering to say any form of goodbye. Casey watched his brother as he became nothing more than a blur, blending into the red brick of the converted school building. Only when Ms. Mazzanno and Walter disappeared into the building did Casey turn the keys in ignition and drove away.

~

He was late. If it only hadn't taken Walter so long to get ready… Whatever. He was here now, and it seemed that his tardiness had gone unnoticed.

Gene McGuinness stood as tall as Casey's shoulders. He was a stout, squirmy man with a lot to say. His portly cheeks were adorned with a roughly shaven beard, greyed from age. He was only fifty, but like a lot of the people in Westport he seemed to be looking rather worse for wear. The workers of the International Southern Marine Tuna Plant stood in a group before him and Casey, as Gene did the roll call. It was just like grade school all over again.

"Hector Lewis." Gene read aloud, not bothering to look up from his clipboard.

"This sucks chief." He replied.

Hector was in his late 20's, he had been working with the plant since he was sixteen years old. His parents had moved here in the late sixties, moving off the Native-American Indian reservation. He was adorned with tattoos, from the neck down and wore his mullet like the old Billy Cyrus.

Gene ignored him and marked Hector present. Casey smiled at him. Hector returned the gesture, but he couldn't quite remove the slight envy from his eyes.

"When you all stop covering each other's asses things will go back to the way they were. Work needs to get done around here and each and everyone of you needs to pull their weight. 'Till then welcome to Alcatraz kids!"

There was a slight murmur of protest from the workers but Gene only grinned and handed the clipboard over to Casey.

"Now?" Casey whispered over his shoulder, the sudden press of responsibility taking him like a shy school kid.

Gene raised his eyebrows unamused.

"Achem." Casey cleared his throat. "Alright. Julia Griffin." He shouted.

Julia smiled at him with a slight tilt of her head. "Here."

Casey spared her a quick glance before averting his gaze back to the list. Julia withheld her excitement at seeing him up there. She was so proud of him, he had been working harder than anyone these past years and he truly deserved the promotion.

"Bunks?" Gene gave Casey a nudge. "Oh sorry. William Bunker."

"Only pigs and judges call me William!" He shouted from the back of the crowd. Which inevitably elicited a series of chuckles and smirks. He stood well taller than most of the workers yet he was gaunt and scrawny with hollow-eyes, his hair had started thinning when he was thirty, that was twenty years ago. Bunks was the walking example of abandoned dreams.

"Yeah, we all know that Bunks. You don't need to remind us again." Casey replied with a hint of sarcasm.

More laughter rung through the room and some of Bunk's friends gave him a pat on the shoulder, ruffling his hair and teasing him. Meanwhile, Gene stood like scarecrow looking disapproving as ever.

Casey reached the end of the list.

"Alright. Everyone who has been given overtime, their names are up on board. Don't be late guys, enjoy the day."

The workers disbanded, their murmured conversation rose as they began to disperse to their areas.

"Hold on!" Gene announced.

Everyone stopped in their tracks and turned back towards Gene and Casey.

"Management would like to officially confirm that Mr. Casey Treggar has been appointed as Assistant Supervisor. He will be overseeing a number of teams as he transitions into my role."

Casey nodded his head and forced an apprehensive smile as everyone applauded him, a couple of his good friends cheering, including Julia.

Gene gave him a pat on the shoulder.

"Attaboy!" He jeered. "Casey, we see a great future for the plant, with you in charge." Gene turned to the crowd as their adulation grew, celebrating not only Casey's promotion but rejoicing that 'Ding-dong' the wicked witch of Gene was dead. "Isn't it great?" he added, "Roll-call was all his idea!"

The clapping faded and the room became silent. Casey was evidently uncomfortable at that revelation, but Gene was as chirpy as ever.

"Alright, get to work!" Gene yelled as he pulled Casey over to the side. "You are here to maximize productivity, never forget that. It is *us* vs *them*. Understand?"

"Yes, Mr. McGuinness." Casey replied quietly.

Gene squinted his eyes in suspicion, then gestured for Casey to follow him. As the neophyte trailed after his superior like an obedient dog, he caught Julia laughing and joking with the packing supplier Dave. Casey suppressed the bolt of jealousy that rose, and continued his stride, ignoring her completely. He maintained his focus on Gene, reminding himself that it was all different now, he was no longer a worker, from here on it would be 'us' against 'them'.

~

Casey flicked and spun an empty cigarette pack between his fingers, the familiar living room couch offered little comfort. The stuffing had long since been packed down and it was littered with stains. The couch had been around since before Casey was born, it was almost as old as the house walls which surrounded it. The crickets sang wildly outside as the moon began to appear behind distant clouds. A light tapping came from the front door and something jumped in Casey's chest. He casually got up and opened the door. There was no need to check who it was, he had been waiting for her all night.

Julia strode into the room like she owned the place, immediately removing her light jacket and shawl.

"Hey." Casey said, slightly taken aback as she walked right past him into the living room.

She turned and winked at him. "Hey stud. I can't stay long tonight. Patrick has softball."

"Got it." He replied, then suddenly remembering he continued. "I got those candles you were talking about."

He motioned with his head to a pair of fancy scented candles wrapped in tiffany blue ribbons. They sat invitingly over the inactive fireplace. Casey walked towards them, but was interrupted after a couple steps.

"No. Not tonight. Just turn the lights off."

Casey stopped mid stride. Julia began to remove her clothes with surprising efficiency. He watched her for a moment, then went to complete her request. Casey wasn't in the best of moods, and whilst he walked towards the wall switch, he let his jealousy take rein over his words.

"So how long have you been hitting on Dave?"

Julia looked unamused at Casey over her shoulder.

"Really Case?"

He didn't respond.

"I already have a jealous wife at home, Casey. I don't need another one here."

He raised his eyebrows as if to say 'fine.' Then turned off the lights and set to undressing himself.

"You're going to have to rock my world quick. Supervisor." She winked again.

Casey was halfway through removing his buttons when he suddenly felt Julia's soft breasts against him. She grabbed his face with both her hands and pressed her lips into his. Suddenly unbuttoning himself became less of a priority and he pulled her aggressively by her hips towards him. Their breaths turned heavy as their tongues ran intricate poetry along each other's lips. Julia's hands moved away from his face, grazing her nails down his chest, all the way down to his belt buckle. It was undone in moments as he grabbed a chunk of her hair, pulling it teasingly. She moaned and Casey's pants were around his ankles a moment later.

"Take me." She whispered into his ear. "Go wild, stud!"

This made Casey's blood run. He tore off his shirt and kicked-off the nuisance of his pants, all the while keeping his lips in motion with hers. God, his heart was pounding, tidal waves of emotion were lapping fourth towards Julia. She met him with equal magnitude. He grabbed her by the soft moon of her buttocks and pulled her up onto him, impaling her on his spear. She wildly wrapped her legs around his waist and they stumbled together in the moonlight towards the couch. When he finally threw her down, Julia smiled as her legs parted wider and Casey took her, under the frozen smiles of family images that observed from the mantle. The loud crash of the ocean drowning out the sounds of their love making.

~

Casey had to refrain from pulling out a cigarette as he sat against the old couch naked. The echoes of Julia's moans swam through his memories, the way she pulled his eyes to hers when he was inside her, the way her soft lips felt against him. He stared blankly at the shelf of photos before him.

He was alone.

Julia had left hours ago.

His eyes focused on a single framed picture. It was Casey as a young boy with his father on *The Majestic*. There was so much pride and joy in that photo. It was the same day that… that Walter had gone overboard. Sounds of cheering and the celebratory brass trumpets intertwined and overcame Julia's sultry breaths, as if a new current had cut in. In light of everything that had happened since, the sounds fell empty and echoed eerily in the recesses of his mind. They stretched amongst the framed pictures of Walter and Casey, they danced colorless against absent walls, and following the weight of what drew them, settled in June's empty bedroom. It was untouched, the bed made neatly, not a thing out of place whilst dust danced in the moonlight and had even settled in thin layers over sheets and the bedside lamps.

Casey wasn't sure when he finally managed to collapse into his own bed. The night hours had drawn by like mist or fog. Unsteady dreams rocked on from the turbulent waves and dragged Casey deep into a soundless sleep, in some mercy, so he may escape what lay at the surface of his own stresses. But, moonlight shines even on stormy nights, her pull is not always the promise of silvery love, but the revelation of greater shadows.

The phone rang. It rang in five cycles before a weary-eyed Casey fumbled along the dresser beside his bed with slightly tingled fingers, numb from deep slumber.

Blindly he answered.

"Hello?"

"Casey?"

"Walt?"

"I can't breathe."

Casey sat up quickly, alarm and panic lighting up his body, reeling in energy from such chthonic whispers.

"What? Walt, are you okay?"

"Call the cops."

A muffled male voice found its way to Casey's ear amidst Walters words.

"Walter, go back to bed!" The distant words formed.

"No, you go back to bed! You sick prick!" Walter screamed as if blood were tinged in the air.

"Get him down!"

There was commotion and havoc. Casey heard the phone drop and several other thuds and scuffling noises.

"Take him down!" The voice came more urgent and aggressive than the last time.

"Back-off asshole!" Walter screamed, fighting with every limb in his body.

"Walter! Walter?" Casey tried to make himself heard, but the phone lay abandoned, dangling over the sterile floors of the ward. His tinny voice went unnoticed as more staff members and security wrestled Walter to the ground. "Walter?"

Then the phone cut out instantly and Casey was left with the high-pitched drone of a disconnected line.

"Dammit!" Casey whispered to himself and he hopped out of bed, throwing on his clothes that were cast on the floor before him. He scrambled out of the house and drove into the starless night, diving-in once again to save his brother.

CHAPTER THREE

asey pulled into the group-home's hospital ward. He cursed as the blaring of ambulance and police lights left blotches in his eyes. *Where was Walter? Was he okay?* Were the only two things that ran through the worried brother's mind. Hastily he unbuckled his seatbelt and jogged over to the somber scene, his truck door slamming behind him. Casey's face whitened as he finally arrived before the entourage of staff members and police workers.

Walter lay unconscious, strapped to a stretcher. One of the male staff members was reciting an account to Officer Griffin, his eye adorned with purple bruising. A paramedic turned to acknowledge Casey as he strode up, and Casey didn't hesitate to introduce himself.

"I'm his brother."

They locked eyes for a moment.

"He was asking for you."

"Can I get in there?" Casey gestured towards the back of the ambulance where two paramedics were now hoisting Walter into.

"We just turned out the lights. You should just call the hospital in the morning."

"Can I follow you in my car?"

"Believe me, he's going to be out all night. A'int nothing waking him up."

Casey spotted empty vials and a syringe in the ambulance.

"You're better off going home, visiting him in the morning."

Casey finally relented, "Okay, got it. Thanks."

The paramedic closed the doors to the ambulance, Walter's resting face could be seen through the small back windows of the vehicle. Casey observed his brother, he couldn't help but feeling sorry for him, Walter had been a magnet for this kind of situation as a moth was to a flame. But like all siblings on this planet they were bound by blood and Casey had to be there by his side. Officer Griffin stepped away from the hospital staff member with his notepad and made his way back to his police cruiser. The paramedic held a bloody rag to his nose and gave Casey a disapproving shake of the head.

"Is he alright?" Casey inquired with another paramedic who stood nearby.

The one he had been speaking with earlier had maneuvered around the ambulance and sat himself in the front passenger seat, filling out the required paperwork. Casey observed him scribbling notes furiously on a clipboard in the side mirror.

"It's broken." He turned to face the injured man. "Looks like you'll be riding with us.

The caretaker nodded and let the paramedic escort him to the ambulance.

"Hey. My brother's sorry, he didn't mean it." Casey offered.

The staff member only glared before hopping into the ambulance.

"Akhem." The clearing of a throat sounded behind Casey. "You're his brother?"

It was Officer John Griffin, Julia's husband. Casey ignored the guilt he felt and faced the man whose wife he was sleeping with.

"Is he in trouble?"

Officer Griffin raised his eyebrows and gave Casey an uncertain stare.

"Walter's lucky that this man's decided not to press charges." Motioning towards the ambulance. "But, they refuse to let him stay here anymore. They want him taken back to his institution in Seattle."

Casey looked up and away, sighing heavily. The officer's gaze met Casey with sympathy.

"You work up at the plant, right?"

Casey nodded. "Yeah. Doesn't half this town?"

Office Griffin smiled and nodded, "My wife's up there too."

"Mm." Casey managed to answer.

"He has a history of this sort of thing, doesn't he?" Officer Griffin went on, back on task.

Casey just continued to nod slowly. "He blacks out, loses control. It's…Hypoxia. He forgets what he does during these states. He's been like this since we were little. Doesn't remember a thing when he wakes up."

Officer Griffin offered him a soft-hearted smile. "Let's see what we can do."

He gestured with his hand and walked towards the building where several staff members watched the spectacle like night owls.

When he wasn't hiding behind his badge or feeding off the power it wielded, John Griffin could be a decent man, Casey gave him that much. He followed him to the awaiting staff to face the music whilst the ambulance carrying Walter and the wounded caretaker wailed off into the night.

~

Casey hurried across the plant entrance. He was late, the previous evening had yielded little sleep, and he had been caught up with Officer Griffin and the hospital administrators for most of it. He hadn't had time to shower and he appeared as if he had just rocked-up from spending years, lost in the wilderness. His hair was disheveled and clothes dry with sweat and anxiety.

The sign above the single story, cinder block building read "Southern Marine Tuna. Est. 1910." Already the smell of the sea was thick in his nostrils, and finding a warm home in the pockets of pores on his skin, and in the fabric of his clothes. It was the sort of smell that grabbed one tight and never really left.

Casey found his way to the dry room. What was mainly empty now, was normally full to the brim at the beginning and end of each workday. This was where assembly line workers went to change and store their belongings. Tiled in white and littered with patches of grey concrete, it was largely unkept, and quite typical of a worker's changing room. Even though he had been promoted, Casey had to house his belonging with his old co-workers, whilst he was training.

Casey opened his locker and was immediately hit by the stench of rotting fish heads, he stared at the offal shaking his head, it was payback for roll-call, he clenched his jaw and pushed them out before grabbing his trainee manager's white coat and a deodorant, shutting the locker door behind him. He slipped on his coat mid-stride and clipped his ID to a neatly ironed breast pocket. The final straggle of workers mingled in the back, occupied in idle conversation with one another. Resentment was evident as they stopped their conversation, exchanging subtle glances with one another as they noticed Casey, he nodded briefly at them as he doused himself in deodorant, they nodded back politely, some tried their best not to snigger or laugh at the fish-heads prank but the dam burst as soon as Casey left their sight and laughter bellowed. Casey rolled his eyes and continued outside, a line in the sand had been drawn.

The elevator always took ages to get from one floor to the next. Casey stood impatiently tapping his foot, hands buried deeply in his pant pockets. Him and a gaggle of workers were herded together like penguins. All of them watched Casey in one way or another, either from the corner of their eyes or blatantly outright. Julia was one of them, and Casey felt her gaze the strongest. He met her stare for a brief second, but quickly turned away not arise suspicion. Julia recognized it for what it was and let her attention drift elsewhere.

The majority of the people around him were his subordinates, other than two managers who stood occupied in conversation closer to the doors. Julia was right next to Casey, but they appeared no more than strangers to the onslaught of onlookers. Julia slightly amused by their charade spindled a piece of fabric off Casey's shirt.

He immediately turned to her, shooting her a sharp glance, as if to say 'what the fuck are you doing.' She held out the small piece of string and smiled wordlessly at him. A disgruntled huff escaped Casey's nostrils.

He knew what she was playing at and had no patience for her games, especially this morning.

The elevator dinged. Casey and the two managers in front of him stepped out, leaving Julia and the rest of the workers trailing with only their stares. However, just when the doors were about to close Julia stepped out.

"I heard about Walter."

Surprised, Casey's eyes snapped back in her direction. The elevator shut and rattled on its way. They were on the assembly floor and the plant was in full swing. The loud hum and swing of machinery, was an orchestra, accompanied by shouts and orders. It was littered with workers either stationed at the assembly line or moving packed fish to inventory and cold storage. Casey stared at her without saying anything. Julia was smart, and her female instincts picked up exactly on what Casey was feeling.

"I can help. Patrick has been…"

But her words were cut off as Casey looked away. Sure enough, Gene was striding across the plant floor, gunning directly for him. Casey steeled himself and shoved Julia and Walter out of his mind.

"You're late hot shot!" Gene announced over the commotion of movement and noise. His beady eyes darted back and forth between Julia and Casey.

"Sorry, Gene. A… Family issue came up."

"Look we all have families. We just don't bring them here. I want you to be on time. Lead by example."

"Yes, Mr. McGuinness. Sorry. It won't happen again."

The plant supervisor held Casey's look, making sure he understood. He turned and met Julia with his prying eyes.

"Is there something we can do for you, Mrs. Griffin?"

Julia politely smiled and shook her head. She took one last glance at Casey then made her way to her colleagues on the assembly line. Gene furrowed his eyebrows confused and his chin came in slightly towards his neck. The man had obviously thought the interaction strange. She had to be more careful about when they spoke to each other. But, Gene just shook it off and returned to the business at hand.

"Alright. Today I want you doing line evaluation. The goal here is to determine worker productivity based on the total amount each shift packs. Let's see those math skills, Treggar."

Casey gave an understanding nod.

~

Walter stared up at the hospital room ceiling. He was still restrained, his arms and ankles strapped to the bed rails with leather straps. He had come to his senses in the early hours of the morning. There had been a struggle as he realized his situation, and he had fought and screamed for a couple hours, demanding that they untie him. He wasn't going to hurt anyone. He knew it. But, of course, based on his behavior last night the hospital staff weren't prepared to take any chances.

Eventually he settled down and had been quiet ever since. Every now and then a nurse would come in to check on him, but his gaze remained fixed on the ceiling. There was the sound of footsteps nearing, and they stopped at the entrance to his room, which had been left open.

Casey appeared in the frame, his tie loose and top button undone. Walter didn't turn to look. Casey hesitated in the doorway before finally approaching his brother.

"Walt."

Walter remained motionless.

Casey followed his gaze to the ceiling which revealed nothing of particular interest. He sighed.

"What's wrong?"

There was a slight hesitation, then Walter spoke.

"Nothing. That's the problem Casey."

More silence.

I lie here quietly, like a good little boy, and anyone who walks past asks 'what's wrong' or 'you ready to comply' or 'you okay?' I do nothing. *Nothing.* And people think I have a problem."

"Walt… Do you remember what happened last night? Do you have any idea why you're here?"

Walter went quiet. There was nothing to discuss.

"You broke his nose. You attacked that poor guy who was just working his shift, up at the group home."

Walter turned away from Casey, ashamed and in denial.

"I don't remember… doing that."

Casey looked at him doubtfully, but pressed on.

"Then tell me what happened." The machine beeped next to Walter. "Y'know, they want to send you back."

Walter's head snapped towards Casey, his face riddled with objection. Walter tried to recount even a second of last night's events, but nothing came to him. The last thing he remembered, he was in his room getting ready for bed, then… Then it went all blank. He had no idea how he had gotten here, or what guy Casey was talking about. Walter deflated and looked back towards the ceiling.

"Just leave me alone then."

"Do you remember calling me?"

"No. Did I?"

"You called me in the middle of the night. Said you couldn't breathe."

Walter scrunched his eyes rubbing them with his index finger and thumb. He couldn't remember a damned thing.

"Are they sending me back?"

Casey took a good long stare at the state of his brother. Strapped and restrained like a wild animal. Casey examined every feature in Walter's face, and took a moment before he spoke. God. He hoped what he was about to say wasn't going to end up biting him in the ass.

"They were. They were about too." Walter's eyes darted over to Casey's. "*But...* I agreed to look after you."

"You did?" Walter stared perplexed, that wasn't characteristic of the Casey he knew.

"Your case worker obviously thought that we should talk about it first."

"Aren't we doing that?"

Casey smiled. "Look, if this is going to work, there have to be rules. Boundaries."

"Like what?"

"Well firstly, you can't go wandering off whenever you want, like you always do. And, you have to go into a day program while I'm at work."

"Okay. What day program?"

"I've pulled some strings with a friend and I can get you a spot at… Well, the only place that was available and willing to help out was… Team Teen."

Walter looked almost aghast. "Crazy scouts?!"

"It's integrated treatment for troubled youths, and they do a bunch of really fun things during the day."

"I know what Team Teen is Case."

Walter was obviously not pleased with the outcome, but it was better than going back to the institution in Seattle. He made a show in front of Casey of not being pleased, but didn't offer any rebuttal.

"Look… If you can't handle this."

"Hmm. Gee, let me think about it. You know how much I love hospitals, this is a hard choice, brother."

Casey was in no mood for jokes.

"Just get me out of here. Please."

Casey went to speak but paused just as the words were about to come out. Was this really the best option. Walter, sensing his brother's hesitation, continued to plead his case.

"I won't get into trouble. Honestly. Thank you, Casey."

"Alright. And don't get confused, Walt. I want to be completely upfront with you. I'm doing this for mom. For some reason she really wants you to be here. I can't possibly imagine why."

Walter dismissed Casey's remark, his focus was untying his shackles, he made an effort to pull his arms up but came short as the leather ties bound him to the side of the bed.

"Okay. First things first, can you get me out of these damn straps."

Casey shook his head, still mid-smile, he motioned to the door, signaling he was leaving.

"Yeah, let me see what I can do about that. Why don't I grab a sandwich in peace, really think about everything? Hang tight buddy."

Walter was taken aback for a moment before he read the smile inching its way up Casey's cheeks. Then, the two brothers managed to laugh, even through all that had just occurred. Casey freed Walter from the straps and helped him up, Walter sprung from the bed and marched to the door, still in the hospital gown that exposed his underwear to the world. "Let's go, before they change their mind." Walter remarked holding the door open, Casey chuckled as he stuffed Walter's belongings in a disposable bag and followed his brother out to freedom.

~

The brothers pulled-off the main beach road and into the driveway of their mother's house around dinner time. The lights of Westport shone through the clear night. Walter, who by now had shed his hospital garb for his own clothes, clutched his duffle bag close to his body as they exited the truck and made their way to the double screen door of the single-story home. Moths flittered around the buzzing light that shone above the welcome mat.

"Still never fixed that light." Walter stated more than questioned.

"Come on, it has its own charm."

"I'd prefer if I didn't feel like there were bugs in my head when I entered a house."

"Bugs in *your* head, really Walt? That's like crazy calling the world cuckoo"

Casey just smiled and shook his head. This could work. This could actually work, he didn't know why he had been so worried.

"I take it I don't have to show you to your room."

Casey threw the keys on the table by the door. It was stacked with old mail and bills that he had yet to sort through.

"No don't worry, I think I'll manage." Walter played along.

His room was sparsely furnished, it was the skeletal remains of what used to be a teenager's quarters. Walter felt like he was stepping into a time machine. Band posters and memorabilia still hung loosely on the wall with tape. Even his old childhood blanket was folded up neatly at the end of the bed, which was smaller than he remembered. He dumped his duffle bag by the footboard and traced his fingers over the small armoire before sitting down.

Walter bounced up and down a couple times, testing the mattress's comfort.

"So, how does it feel to be back?"

Casey appeared in the doorway.

Walter took a moment to reflect. "You know what… it feels good." Casey raised his eyebrows. "Feel just like a time machine. We're back, Casey. Back to the nightmare."

Casey nodded smiling, he tossed a relic of a cell-phone in his direction. "It's old, but works."

Walter examined it, it was one of those early flip-top models, but he didn't care. It was a phone.

"Where's your bag?" Casey demanded.

Walter gestured with his eyes and Casey picked it up, placing it on a dresser and removing an entourage of medication bottles, clothing and a beautiful set of rosary beads. He neatly placed the beads on the top of an adjacent dresser next to one of Walter's old stuffed animal toys, Mr. Pelty, a vintage stuffed bear with a little blue jacket.

Walter just watched as Casey read the label on each of his medication bottles.

"You're supposed to take one…" Casey squinted at the fine print. "After each meal."

"I can read you know."

Casey shook the rest of the bag out onto the floor just to make sure it was empty. A couple aerosol containers fell out, various deodorants and such. Walter tried to look as neutral as possible when Casey stood speechless, the bag still in his hand.

"Walter. What are these?"

"Deodorants. They help people smell nice you know, keep the odor away."

Casey dropped the bag burying his face in his hands for a second.

"What the hell? I thought you were through with this junk."

"I am. I just like how they feel." He paused. "It feels nice."

"Whatever."

Casey stared at him like a worried parent before throwing the cans back into the bag.

"Okay. What else am I forgetting."

"To put my diapers on?"

Casey was exhausted and unamused so he just ignored the comment.

"Tomorrow, you have to check in at the day program. Dr. McKenzie is going to be monitoring you throughout, see if you're a good fit. So be on your best behavior."

Walter nodded slowly, appearing resigned, but he had no other option, it was this or a one-way ticket back to Seattle. Casey could read his brother like a book by now and it was obvious that he wasn't excited about the arrangement.

"When… will all this end for me, Casey?"

The words lingered and permeated long after they had been spoken, the brothers felt the stigma that had drowned their family and once again, had reduced them to silence.

"Get some sleep, Walt. I'll see you in the morning."

Casey quietly got up and turned off the lights as he left. Walter didn't bother taking off his clothes as he got under the covers. He listened to his brother get ready for bed and waited until all noises had ceased and he was sure that Casey was asleep. Then, Walter slipped a photo out of his pocket. His mother and father stood smiling together under a tree with the ocean in the background. Walter took out a torch and huddled under his comforter. The faces of his parents swirled around in his mind. They both looked so young and carefree, so much had changed in the last fifteen years. The memory of that day began to rise up. A silver haired doctor examining him with June standing by his side. Walter switched-off the torch and closed his eyes. Not now, he couldn't think about this now. He lay under the covers with his own breath for a long time before the mercy of sleep took him over.

CHAPTER FOUR

—— ◆◇◆ ——

Amiddle aged, rather heavy-set woman was leading Casey and Walter through the halls of the Team Teen building. Walter took note particularly at her name tag 'Lana', the Program Director. Walter shut his eyes and mouthed her name repeatedly, "Lana.. lana.. lana.". Casey stared sternly at Walter, he discreetly shook his head, they could not jeopardize this arrangement. The Program Director lightly frowned at Casey, catching the end of his interaction with Walter. Casey deflected it with a polite smile and focused on her as she continued.

"This is our arts room."

The party of three stood outside a rather colorfully decorated room. There were a group of teenagers laughing and working together on an arts and craft project.

"Great work Tracie! I love what you did with the collage."

A soft encouraging voice came from the activities leader. She was a young, pretty woman with hazel hair. Upon seeing her Walter wondered that maybe this wouldn't be so bad, she could be the silver lining to this entire ordeal.

The day program director continued speaking to the brothers from outside in a low murmur as to avoid disturbing the kids inside.

"We have arts and crafts every Monday and Friday morning. And on Tuesday and Thursday it gets a bit more physical. We like to have sport activities followed by 'express yourself' which is when the teenagers get to sing along with a music therapist."

She turned to Walter and spoke to him as if he was a five-year-old child.

"Do *you* like music, Walter?"

He exchanged a disapproving look with Casey. "Yeah, but not your kind."

"Walt. Don't be rude."

The day program director put on a sickly-sweet smile.

"Oh, that's okay. What do you like to listen to, then?"

"Death Metal. Prison rap."

"Oh my. You're right. That is not my kind of 'get-down' at all, but we've got someone here who likes that."

Walter frowned at Casey. Did someone actually like that, he was joking. Casey let out a little smirk, shaking his head. Lana, the program director ticked a couple of boxes on a sheet of paper.

"How about hobbies? What do you like to do for fun?" Lana inquired.

"Not much."

"Hmm." She looked up and down the form. "Well, I've got a whole list of activities here…"

Walter grabbed the list out of her hands.

"Oh." Lana was rather taken aback by his forwardness.

He flipped it around and inspected every activity on it.

"I like fishing, sailing and boats."

Lana's expression was replaced by a smile.

"Ahh wonderful!" She scribbled his answers down on the paper. "Wow, you are officially our outdoorsman!"

"Great. Do I get a sticker?"

She nodded, overjoyed to see that she was getting through to him. Casey smiled and patted Walter on the shoulder.

"Alright shall we move on? I want to show you the playground."

Walter rolled his eyes at Casey which triggered another smirk.

~

Casey pulled in late again to work again. It had taken longer than he had expected to fill out all the paperwork for Walter, which included release forms, wavers and other administrative requirements. Roger, an old manager looked up from his stack of papers as Casey approached him. He took a sparing glance at the clock hanging on the wall before handing Casey a clipboard.

"Thanks Roger." He looked around before whispering, "Does Gene know I'm late?"

"Sorry Casey" Roger shrugged. "He came down here earlier."

"Shit! Thanks anyway."

Casey turned to leave when he locked eyes with Gene up in the skywalk. He staring down at him like a hawk, waiting for its prey.

~

Walter sat rather uncomfortably on the ground. The therapist had arranged them on cushions in a circle. It had been many years since Walter stopped being able to cross his legs, and his knees were high in the air, his hips tightly wound. A young girl named Sarah was sitting directly opposite him and she spoke slowly, all emotion and inflection a distant concept to her blunt tone. It was as if she were reading her life off a list.

"After that, they served my mom papers and then people came and took me away a couple days later."

"Do you still have any contact with your birth parents?"

"No…"

A heavy weight settled on the room as something like sorrow and grief filled her eyes.

"Do you have any kids Dr. Marsh?"

The therapist smiled and nodded his head. The conversation didn't go further than that though,

"Thank you for sharing Sarah." He made direct eye contact with her before turning to address the rest of the group. "Sarah's story is about coping with loss. Maybe some of you can relate to this?"

The room went quiet and many people avoided Dr. Marsh's gaze, each of them lost in the revere of their past. Walter however stared blankly at the ceiling.

"Walter do you have anything to share?"

"What?"

He snapped out of his daydreaming and returned to the room slightly puzzled.

"We're talking about obstacles. Have you ever felt that you conquered something difficult or challenging?"

"No."

"Really? I highly doubt that. Maybe you should take the time to think about it."

Dr. Marsh gave Walter the space to mull it over. The room sat in silence and all eyes were on him. Finally, mainly to avoid all the attention on him, Walter spoke.

"In fifth grade, there was this kid here that called me names like 'nigger', 'coon', and 'spooky' etc. I'm obviously not." He gestured to his Caucasian-ness for the whole room to see. "He must have heard me listening to N.W.A or Cube, or something. So, one day I finally had enough of the name calling, plus it was rude to the kids and teachers who were actually black."

"Ahh yes this is a perfect example." Dr. Marsh stated. "Please go on."

"So, this one day I went up to him and thought about educating him, but he was brick-stupid and a racist, so I just punched him square in the face. I split his lip open, and he had to get stitches right here."

Walter pointed to a place on his lip. Several of the teenagers perked up, as if this was the first interesting thing they had heard all year. Dr. Marsh's composure didn't change even the slightest in light of Walters story. He was a professional after all.

"Do you think that punching him was a good way to work out your differences?" The doctor scribbled something down on a piece of paper as he spoke, his eyes not leaving Walter's for a second.

"Well, sometimes you need to hit difficult or challenging, in order to make it… disappear. He never bothered me again, so yes I'd say that was a good way to deal with it."

A male across the room began to laugh. 'Patrick Griffin' was written in sharpie on the name tag sticker pasted to his shirt. Walter smiled back at him. Meanwhile, Dr. Marsh sighed, continuing to note things down.

~

It was the end of the workday. Casey, Julia, Dave, and Hector stood smoking cigarettes in a semi-circle nearby Casey's truck. The sun was still in the sky, slowly making its descent below the horizon, bathing everything in a wash of orange and purple.

"I get the same as you guys. Trust me."

"No way you do. Stop messing with us man."

"I'm still training, Hec."

"Yeah, but still. A promotion means more money. If it were me, I'd want Gene's salary. What's he take home?"

"Yeah, what does Gene even really do?" Dave chimed in.

Before Casey could answer Hector cut in again.

"Nothing. He walks around with his pad jerking off, while we gut fish all day."

Casey shook his head as he blew out smoke.

"He does a lot. Trust me."

"He ain't here man, you can be yourself, stop kissing his ass."

Casey didn't respond, Hector saw this as an opening to probe deeper.

"So, when are you gonna get us that overtime? You know we're all aching for double pay. The current work climate ain't too good on us Case, you know that."

Casey smiled, shaking his head.

"That goes through Gene."

"Yeah sure it does." Hector smiled back.

"Anyway." Hector directed his attention to Dave. "You ready?"

"Yeah." Dave replied.

Hector flicked his cigarette to the ground, blowing out the final puff and grinded the embers into the ground with his boot.

"Later guys." Dave bid Julia and Casey farewell, whilst Hector threw a goodbye over his shoulder with his right hand, sparing one final glance at Casey and Julia before taking off. The two of them didn't say anything for a while, until Hector and Dave were long gone.

"Are you going out with them later?" Julia finally said.

"I don't know. Don't think so."

"Might be good for you to get out. A change of pace."

"Maybe. Maybe I'll take Walt with me. 'Hi guys, you remember my brother. He's a great guy, but if he blacks out and beats the hell outta you, please don't sue and try to be understanding'."

Julia gave him a sympathetic smile.

"I think you should still take him. He'll like it."

Casey shrugged her off. 'Maybe' he said in his silent words, before throwing his cigarette to the ground. Julia hesitated, then spoke what was on her chest.

"I miss my stud."

That took him by surprise. Casey turned to face her. A little smile formed across his lips.

"That reminds me."

Casey maneuvered around her and opened up the passenger seat door to his car. He reached into the glove compartment and pulled out a small gift bag.

"Here." Casey held out the offering.

She paused, looking around to make sure no one was watching.

"For Walt. For getting him into Pat's group. Thank you, I don't know what I would've done without your help."

"It's fine." She said. "Really."

Julia still hadn't taken the gift from his hand and Casey was starting to get offended. He pushed it towards her again and this time Julia politely accepted it and quickly shoved it into her lunch box.

"I'll open it later."

Casey understood her reservation and he smiled a half broken, heart sinking smile. He often forgot she was leading a whole other life. She was the one risking everything by being with him. She was the one who had to hide from her family.

"You want me to come by tomorrow?" She asked from the corner of her eyes.

"Yeah." Julia smiled as he continued. "I'd like that."

He watched her walk off towards her small yet reliable car. There was a baby on board sticker on the back window and a couple stuffed animals from when Patrick was a child. Julia gave him a sultry smile as she cruised past him and out of the lot. It was the smile that caught him in the first place, one that made his whole heart sink and leap at the same time. He found that his lips were upturned as well. She had a way of moving his emotions that honestly scared the man. He didn't want to be so bound to her, so powerless. Perhaps he would feel differently if he could put a ring on her finger. But, that spot was already taken. God knows if it wasn't, if she didn't have a child… he would turn the whole world over for her.

Casey shoved those feelings down, far, far away. Then he got into his own truck and left in the silence of his own company.

~

It was just past six when the brothers arrived in the all too familiar halls of Westport Memorial Hospital. They were both looking sharp. Even Walter had on a nicely fitting blazer and button up shirt. They were skirting on the boundaries of visiting hours, and the nurse made sure they were aware of it by tapping her watch as they passed.

"We'll be quick." Casey replied.

They rounded the corner to June's room when an unexpected face met them right as they were about to enter the door. She was just leaving.

"Mrs. Stevens?! What a pleasant surprise."

"Casey! Oh my god it's so good to see you. And…It can't be. Walter, is that you?"

Walter gave her a little nod and managed a light smile despite the circumstances of their meeting. Mrs. Stevens's eyes wandered back and forth between the two brothers, noting the concern in their faces, despite their efforts to cover it up. She reached out and touched both of their shoulders.

"Don't you boys worry, June is a tough cookie. She'll pull through."

Walter smiled politely and Casey nodded 'thanks' for her kind words.

"I'll see you both around." Mrs. Stevens said with reassuring eyes before giving them each a kiss on the cheek and leaving.

The boys waited until the sound of her shoes were a distant echo, then Casey stepped forward into his mother's hospital room.

"You mind if I wait out here?"

Casey stopped and turned to face his brother incredulously.

"Yes, I mind, this is our mother."

Walter looked down at the ground.

"Look, I know you don't want to see her like this, neither do I. Let's just do all we can to get her out."

Casey was right, but Walter was still reluctant. He wasn't sure if he could handle seeing her so sickly and frail. Casey took Walter's arm and lovingly dragged him inside. June was still unconscious as Casey went to sit by her side. He held her limp hand in his, as he always did.

"Walt, tell mom you're here."

"She knows."

"Come and sit with us. Ask her, what she wants to tell you."

"I don't know, Case. She's sleeping."

Angrily Casey gestured with his head to the opposite seat beside the bed. Walter began to pale.

"I feel sick. I'll be back."

With that, Walter rushed out of the room, his head low. He managed to make it to the bathroom before throwing up in the bathroom sink. 'God, what's wrong with me', he thought. Casey had every right to be angry at him, something inside was blocking him from connecting with his mother, like an invisible shield. Walter looked at his ghostly reflection in the mirror, a drool of spit still dripping from his lip.

"Dammit! Walter, you reject!" he cursed, trying to gather himself.

He fumbled with the tap letting the cold water run fierce and splashed his face slapping himself lightly on the cheek.

"Come on, buddy. Come on. Get it together."

But the sickly image of his mother would not leave his mind and he gagged again. The fluorescent light of the hospital bathroom flickered and buzzed. His mind began its incessant whispers, like a tiny devil on his shoulder. He wasn't ready to be able to go back. It was better for everyone if he wasn't here. It would have been better if he was never born. His whole life he had been a burden to everyone around him, everyone he loved. The bathroom door swung open as Walter was half braced against the sink, mumbling. He quickly straightened up and adjusted his shirt. A man in plain clothing walked past him without saying anything and locked himself in one of the stalls. Walter let the water run again and splashed his face one last time before exiting.

He did not make his way back to the hospital room as he had indicated to Casey. Instead, keeping his head down, Walter shuffled back to Casey's truck, doing his best to avoid any direct contact with anyone he passed. It was a good thirty minutes before he saw Casey emerge from the automatic, double-sliding doors of the hospital entrance.

Casey said nothing to his brother as he got into the truck. Walter followed suit. Only when they were driving out of the parking lot did Walter speak.

"I'm sorry Casey.

There was a long moment of silence as Casey processed his reply.

"It's just too much for me to handle right now."

Casey lightly smirked, playing out his first response of telling Walter that this wasn't about his narcissistic ass, however the wiser angels in him took the reins.

"I just hope you're ready before it's too late." Casey replied.

The remainder of the ride went on in silence, neither brother spoke. The Grand Tasman Hotel was only a ten-minute drive away, as were most things in town. Right beside the entrance was your typical blue-collar bar. Television sets broadcasted a plethora of sports, horse racing, basketball, golf. The resident barflies were seated at their alter, growlers half-full of beer not far from their hands. Casey lead the way and clapped Hector and Dave on the backs.

"Funny seeing you two jokers here." He bantered.

"Why if it isn't mister supervisor." Dave threw back. "Take a seat." Casey nodded in Walter's direction whilst gesturing to the open chairs beside him. "Glad to see you, Walt." Hector shouted, delighted to see an old friend.

Walter nodded back.

"Two growlers of Adams." Casey ordered from the bartender, who was in the midst of drying a glass with an old cloth. He nodded in acknowledgement and set to pouring a light ale from the tap.

"I was just telling Hector that I gotta put new brakes in Nicki's car, any of yous wanna help?" Dave asked.

"Answer is still no from me." Hector replied.

"Oh come on. I helped you out when that dog attacked Rosie."

"Rosie is my wife Dave. Nicki's your skank, she should be putting brakes on your car."

"Asshole…" Dave muttered.

"Look. Soon as she lands you, and we both know that she will, you're gonna be doing that handyman shit all your life. She gonna be asking you to fix everything left, right and middle."

"You think I can do better than, Nicki?"

Casey chimed in, "With that belly, maybe a Mrs. Claus type, or one of the reindeers?"

Hector cut in, "The slow one, at the back."

A murmur of chuckles resounded. Dave shook his head, taking the jest, he took a big gulp from his glass. the bartender planted the two large growlers in front of Casey and Walter.

"Look, I'm just saying, enjoy the dating part, Dave. While she's still trying to impress you. Once you walk the plank, all that 'mutual stuff' goes out the window. Then you're nothing more to her than her lipstick." Casey added. "Dipstick."

Hector and Casey chuckled, playing off one another like a Vegas act. Walter sat quietly at the end of the bar, slowly sipping his beer. The boys kept talking on the background while Casey leaned over.

"You okay?" He said.

"Yeah, I'm fine." Walter replied, and then added, "How are you?" seeing that Casey wanted more of a response."

"Hey… I don't like seeing her there either. I'm sorry how I acted at the hospital and on the drive down. What I said… it was uncalled for."

Walter nodded into his glass but refrained from speaking.

"Soon as you wanna leave, just let me know. Alright?" Casey assured.

"Okay."

Walter turned his attention to the television. It had just begun to pour outside. The door to the bar opened and a familiar step sounded. Casey turned to see Julia and John removing their raincoats. The couple crossed the room and sat at a table near the bar, right in clear view of the four men.

"There's princess Julia and her Sheriff Studly." Hector said, pointing with his head in their direction.

Casey nodded, "Gotta love, Westport. You can't go anywhere without the entire town showing up.", he took a sip of his beer.

"Should we say hi?" Dave asked.

"Go on. He'll probably put on a big show, then write you a ticket." Hector took a big gulp, "Unlawful hello."

Dave and Hector chuckled.

"I got four speeding fines last month because of him. I was almost past city lines. What kind of leech positions himself there?" Dave vented.

"As they say, big hat; no cattle." Hector mumbled.

Casey ignored their jeering and continued to watch Julia as she passively listened to John. She seemed restless.

"We should go." Casey abruptly announced.

"Why? We haven't seen Walt in years." Hectored protested.

"We got things to do back at the house."

"What things?" Walter intercepted.

"Yeah what things, Case?" Dave pried.

"*Family* things."

"On a Friday night?"

"Does it matter what night it is? We have to go."

The expression on Casey's face said it all and Hector took a step back.

"Alright, take it easy. Walt, it was good to see you, maybe next time we could all go fishing."

Casey ignore him and turned to go, but then came Walter's reply, "Really?"

Fear and panic rushed through Casey hearing Walter's hopeful reply.

"Sure thing. I got the hook-up. Be just like when we were kids." Hector encouraged, smiling and offering a brotherly clap on Walter's shoulder.

"Okay. When?" Walter immediately accepted the offer.

Casey shot Hector a look of cold disapproval.

"What?" Hector feigned.

Casey rolled his eyes, shaking his head in disbelief and turned to leave again.

"Hold up." Hector fished Casey's arm and closed the distance between them so that the next conversation would be just between them. "I need some overtime, put me up this week. With Rosie out of action…"

"Look Hec, I can't help you. Go to Gene."

"Screw Gene!" Hector replied well above a whisper. However, he quickly caught himself and softened his tone with a sigh. "We need it brother. Dave too."

Walter didn't even notice his hands clenching into fists as the tension in the room stretched thin. Looking up, he met eyes with Dave who gave him a reassuring wink. That helped Walter to calm down a bit, his fists loosened. Hector backed up in the same moment, and patted Casey on the shoulder with an overly masculine vigor.

"Atta boy."

"See you both, Monday." Casey uttered, cold and all business.

Both men gave him an expecting nod, but then turned to Walter with softer expressions.

"See ya, Walt." Hector waved.

The brothers left in silence, taking the long way out around the bar.

"What's wrong?" Walter trailed behind him, trying to match his brother's pace.

Casey didn't reply, he needed to get out, anywhere but here. A shout came from behind them.

"Hey Walter!"

The voice stopped both brothers in their tracks, Casey recognized it and his blood rushed. Walter on the other hand look puzzled and confused as he turned to face Officer Griffin.

"How are you feeling?"

"Fine. Do we know each other?"

Casey muttered a curse under his breath then turned around to meet everything he had been avoiding.

"We met briefly the other day. At the group home." John said.

Walter understood what that meant.

"Well, it's good to see you again, I guess. In better circumstances." Walter replied with whatever little dignity he could muster up. "This is my brother, Casey."

"We met as well." The officer replied.

Casey threw together a makeshift smile in John's direction. The door to the female bathroom opened up and Julia stepped right into the three of them.

"Oh! Hello, it's not often you walk out of a bathroom and into a group of three fine gentlemen." She said.

"This is my wife, Julia."

"Hello." Walter said whilst shaking her hand.

Casey nodded in her direction. "Southern Marine, right?"

"Yeah that's right." She smiled, "I've seen you around, here an' there."

"Why don't y'al sit with us for a drink. What do you think Jules?"

"That… sounds like a great idea." She said, still smiling in Casey's direction.

Casey on the other hand didn't find this situation amusing. In fact, he was doing everything in his power to not lose it right then and there. Walter absentmindedly moved to sit down, but Casey reached out a hand to stop him.

"Sorry we can't. We have a few things to do."

Walter was looking questioningly at Casey yet again, whom shot him a stern look.

"Uh yes." Walter replied meagerly.

"Aw, that's a shame. Some other time then?"

"When?" Walter replied immediately.

There was a moment of awkward silence which was broken by little laughs from Julia and John, who exchanged glances. Walter didn't know what was so funny, and his innocence was endearing to the couple before him.

"Alright time to go Walt." Casey guided his brother's arm.

Walter trailed behind until they were out of the bar, the rain coming down overhead quickly soaked them as they ran towards Casey's truck. It was a relief when the brothers got inside and slammed the doors behind them. Casey let out a huge exasperated sigh and hunched over the steering wheel, banging his head a couple times on its rubber handle.

"No, no, no."

"Case?"

Silence.

"You want to tell me what's going on?" Walter's voice cut through the air and settled. Casey looked at his brother and for the first time felt like some of the weight could be taken-off his shoulders. He turned the keys in the ignition then began to speak as the truck drove away.

By the time they were home and in the living room, every detail had been spilled. Walter was sitting on the couch in a half-distant daze and Casey was pacing slightly, a thin glass of whiskey in his hand.

"How did it even happen?" Walter questioned.

"I don't know… We worked together on the line… We got talking… Then things just happened."

"She's married, Casey."

"God, I know! I know… You don't have to state the obvious, Walt."

"I'm telling Mom."

"What?" Casey scoffed incredulously. "We're adults, you can't tell *mom*. Besides, if you tell, I'll tell her about the guy who's nose you broke."

This rendered some silence from Walter. Casey got lost in his own whirling thoughts for a moment before Walter looked up to his brother.

"Do you love her?"

There was a pause.

"No… Maybe? I don't know."

"Have there been others… like her?"

"What do you mean, older women?" Walter nodded.

"Yeah, here and there. Some older, some not as old." Casey replied with some hesitation.

"Jesus, Casey. Did you go rummaging around in mom's stuff, found her address book and used it to find dates?"

Casey glared back in response which ushered a little smile from Walter. The smile lingered for a couple moments then dramatically shifted to one of worry and disgust.

Reading Walters expression, Casey responded, "What? Why do you look like that?"

"You didn't do it on my bed did you?"

Casey just stared at his brother, but there were no signs of comedy in Walter's eyes.

"Now that you ask… it's the first place we did it."

Walter took that as a 'No'. Casey took a sip of whisky.

"Mom's?"

Casey coughed, bringing the whisky back up. "Oh god, please don't make this weird!"

"Why did you tell me this, Case?"

"Uh well. Because… she's coming for dinner. Tomorrow."

Walter stared, waiting for a smile or anything that revealed Casey was joking. But nothing came.

"Great… Just great." Walter said whilst burying his face in his palms.

"Please be nice."

Walter couldn't make eye contact with his brother, it was too much to process. He was used to the simple chaos of the psych ward. Drama happened every day, but there it was expected, there it was crazy and ridiculous and drowned out with pills. Not to mention he didn't care or bother to make friends with anyone there. But this... This was different. This was his brother, and he was having an affair with a married woman and to make the matters worse she was married to a man who possessed firearms and an over inflated ego. Did his brother just expect him to just sit idly by at dinner and play the nice, friendly mentally-ill patient?

Casey tried to read Walter's unreadable expressions. He was always like that, so blank, so emotionless. But Casey knew that a hive of activity was going on underneath the mask that his brother wore to the world. *What was he thinking?* A sharp uneasiness worked its way through him, and he washed it away with the final kick of his whisky.

CHAPTER FIVE

Steam bellowed from a boiling-pot and the clank of pans and sizzling food all meddled together in the dim light of early evening. Casey was wearing his mother's apron as he stirred a pasta sauce. With each stir the clack of clam shells opening could be heard. Fresh scallops and prawns basted in their own juices and their aroma was making his mouth water. He poured in a little white wine and did a quick jerk of the pan back and forth. The food crackled and sizzled, finally he sprinkled some red chili sparingly over it all.

Casey was so lost in cooking that he didn't even hear Julia enter. She snuck up behind him and put her arms around his waist. Leaning her head and a nuzzling up Casey's neck. He rested his head atop hers and they both smiled, basking in the silence of touch. Julia kissed his ear, she lightly traced her tongue on his ear lobe and gave it a tinny nibble. Casey couldn't fight the fire rising in him as his whole body tingled with the sensation she was offering him.

"Why don't we just skip to desert?" She whispered quietly into his ear. A hint of mischief ran on the undertones of her voice and it made Casey's hair stand-up on end.

Finally, he turned to her and his neck craned like a swan as the two looked at each other, still tied at the hips. Julia started kissing his neck, but Casey hesitated.

"Wait." Casey hesitated which caused Julia to pause. "Walter's here."

Julia took a step back, obviously disappointed. With nothing to do about the situation Casey returned to stirring the sauce. He pulled a string of pasta from the pot to see if it was ready, 'Al dente' to the bite. Not yet he assessed. But Julia was still hung-up on the fact that their evening of passion was going to be interrupted by an unwanted brother.

"Umm. Couldn't you send him to the movies or church or something?"

Casey gave her a judging look, as if to say, 'who are you to suggest that?'.

"He can't go by himself. What if he gets into trouble?"

Julia folded her arms. "Well then Casey, what are *we* supposed to do?"

Casey smiled. "Take a seat madame. I'm cooking for you."

"I've got food at home, thank you."

She was not here for food, that much was clear. Casey looked crushed. His whole posture slumped as the reality of their relationship came into light. He did his best to cover it up, but Casey never was good at hiding his emotions. He quickly tried to put on a poker face but Julia was too observant, she had already knew how he felt.

Julia took the spoon out of his hand and ran an elegant finger down his chest towards his abdomen. Leaning in close to his lips she held them a hair's breadth from his. Casey could practically taste her lip balm.

In a sultry whisper she spoke to him. "I am wearing nothing underneath this little dress."

"Oh, is that so." He replied. "Good."

He took the time to take her in fully. She was wearing a light see-through cheesecloth dress, with delicate embroidery on the neckline and hem. Her form could be seen as plain as day. Suddenly Casey realized that Walt was in the other room.

"Wait. Not good. Hold-on, I'll get you something."

He pulled away and quickly strode to the hall. When he got around the corner, he let out a heavy breath and leaned against the wall, hormones pulsing through him. Julia let out an exasperated sigh and folded her arms to cover her chest as she stood, half-abandoned in the open kitchen. Casey gathered himself and opened the door to his mother's room. The room was still and silent, and for a moment Casey forgot why he was there. He forgot that Julia was waiting and Walter, was one wall over. The familiar old smell that all elders seem to share still lingered in his mother's room. However, here it was hinted with fresh rose and lavender, June's favorite scents. Casey flicked on the light and a hollow ache opened in his chest. He swallowed it down and slowly walked over to the closet. There, neatly arranged was all of June's clothes. He gently let his fingers run down one of her favorite floral dresses. The fabric was soft and worn, and smelt of fabric-softener.

"Casey?"

He quickly turned around, snapped out of his daze. Julia was standing in the doorway. He cleared his throat and pulled out the dress, draping down off a wooden hanger.

"Here you go. This should fit."

Julia didn't say anything but she kept her eyes fixed on Casey's as she walked over, mid stride she removed her dress and stood before him naked. Casey's eyes danced over her milky toned flesh; it was as though he could feel her without touching her. He meekly handed her the dress.

"I better get back to cooking."

With that he left her alone in Junes room and closed the door softly behind him.

The table was set and Walter sat across Julia, silent and uncomfortable. She wore one of his mother's dresses. Lightly she smiled at him as she sipped from one of their mother's wine glasses. The unease was set as much as the cutlery on the table. Casey walked over carrying two steaming plates of spaghetti, fresh with the fruit of the sea. Walter didn't hesitate and began eating, not even waiting for Casey to sit, who was at the stove filling a plate of his own. Once Casey sat between the two bodies Julia picked up her fork and began to pick at her food, nudging clam and scallop here and there, twirling the pasta as her thoughts spun as well. She ate a forkful and chewed. Casey watched her face, and noticing his attention, she forced a smile.

"This is really good. Did your mom teach you how to cook like this?" She said, breaking the silence.

Casey lit up proudly. "Yeah. I guess, I must've just learned by watching her."

He took his seat and unfurled a white napkin on his lap before lifting his fork to eat.

"Mom never made spaghetti." Walter mumbled from the lowly mood, his chest sunk towards his plate.

Casey glared at Walter from the corner of his eyes amidst a thorough chew. Walter met his stare in challenge and purposefully said nothing. Rolling his eyes Casey returned his gaze to Julia.

"Does the dress fit okay?"

Walter inhaled a bite at Casey's question, coughing and spluttering, trying to regain his breath. Immediately embarrassed and slightly ashamed, Julia's face reddened.

"It fits well." She replied politely.

Casey nodded, ignoring Walter. This was fine, everything was okay. They just needed to get through this dinner. He continued to twirl big reels of spaghetti, his plate disappearing almost as fast as Walters'. Julia on the other hand made more of a show of eating, than actually eating. She took little bites here and there, and otherwise nudged the food around with her fork in silence. Casey noticed, but made an effort to make nothing of it, his thoughts had usually spun him in wrong directions and now was not the time to overthink.

No one spoke for a few minutes, but the time stretched on and seemed like years. Julia, unable to bare it any longer broke the silence with a false voice of optimism and curiosity.

"So… What were you boys like as kids?"

Casey and Walter exchanged little glances.

"I don't know." Casey replied. "Quiet."

Julia smiled. "I bet you were adorable."

"Yeah, I guess I was pretty adorable."

She giggled. "What about you Walter?"

He didn't reply immediately, he was too busy slurping-up the spaghetti off his plate, the quicker he finished the quicker he could leave.

Eating like a famished caveman who hadn't seen food for a century. With a full mouth he eventually replied "Not adorable."

"Walter was tough." Casey chimed in, filling the blanks in Walters response. "He was always getting into fights. Always trying to prove himself to our dad."

Julia looked up from her food towards Walter. A thought crossed her mind and she hesitated at first to speak. But in the end, she put her fork down and asked the question many were too afraid to ask, either out of etiquette or fear.

"What happened to you?

The clinking of cutlery on porcelain ceased. For a moment even the moist sounds of chewing mouths fell quiet.

"Too much TV." Walter deflected, not bothering to look up.

The sounds of eating resumed.

Casey forced a smile.

Dabbing his mouth with his napkin Casey once again stepped in to fill the words his brother wouldn't speak.

"Walter got into an accident when we were kids." Julia's eyebrows raised at that. "He almost drowned."

"Oh… I'm so sorry to hear that." Julia replied sympathetically. Which of course Walter took as pity.

He just kept eating, almost at the final stretch. She averted her eyes from him and looked to Casey. It was obvious she had hit a nerve that wasn't quite healed from the wound around it. 'Sorry' she said with her eyes. Casey reached over and took her hand under the table assuring her it was okay. It was not okay however, and everyone at the table knew it, but only Walter appeared brave enough to acknowledge it.

"Casey saved my life." He said. Except there was no tone of gratitude or love within it. It was tinged with sarcasm and irony. "He got a medal an' all."

Julia however, in her discomfort looked at Casey with admiration, missing the telling signs in Walter's inflection.

"Wow. Adorable *and* brave." She winked at him.

Casey shrugged it off with practiced modesty.

Finished with his food, Walter motioned he would like to leave to Casey, who replied "Sit with us for a bit." Reluctant, Walter now watched the two interact. He studied them, narrating their behavior in his head. A strange twisted part of him was amused and fascinated by the dynamic before him. There was Julia, an older woman in his mother's dress, and Casey still young and bearing no sign of age, gazing at her with starlight in his eyes. *Interesting.* Walter thought, Sigmund Freud or even a hack like Dr. Marsh would be in their element here.

Walter must have missed something amidst his internal musings, for Julia pushed away from the table and picked-up her plate which wasn't even half eaten. She dumped the remains into the bin. The work of love and labor slowly slipping from the plate and falling into the trash with a muted thump. The brothers both watched in silence. Walter was obviously disapproving of her waste and made it apparent to Casey in a judgmental gaze. Casey ignored him, as was his practice.

"Can I ask you a question, Julia?" Walter spoke loudly, rendering surprised looks from both his brother and his cheating lover. She was amidst drying her plate with a clean rag.

"Umm. Sure." She replied, looking at Casey and then back to Walter, as if unsure how to answer, perhaps sensing the strangeness of Walter's sudden outgoingness.

"Do you love your husband?"

As if a gunshot had gone off, Julia's emotions spiked dramatically. She had been taken completely off-guard and for a split second her hand slipped on the rag and the plate came crashing on the ground.

Smash!

It splintered into pieces, big chunks and tiny slivers flying across the kitchen floor.

"Walt!" Casey yelled.

"No, don't, it's fine." Julia replied, flustered. "I should be going."

"No, wait." Casey got up and stood between the two, then he turned to Walter with fury written on his face. "Walt! Get out!"

"What?" Walter replied, innocent. "I read an article that eighty percent of women who have affairs do it for self-esteem. After years of marriage they lose self-worth and try to seek it in a younger man. They still love their husbands."

"Out!" Casey ordered again, interrupting Walter mid-spiel.

Walter scoffed at his brother. "Are you really kicking me out of our own kitchen?"

"Out."

Walter got up slowly and left in silence. The tension hung in the air for a while longer, both Casey and Julia stared at the empty seat. Eventually Julia bent down and commenced picking up the broken porcelain, one of a set of plates passed down from his grandmother to his mom, which would eventually go to him and Walter. Julia huffed out a sigh and shook her head. She was angry with herself, angry that she had agreed to this dinner, and angry that she had been so clumsy to drop the damn thing in the first place. Casey bent down and began help her with the mess.

"I'm sorry. He didn't mean… anything." Casey finally said.

Julia looked up and managed a pouty smile. She stopped picking up the broken pieces for a moment, and Casey took the opportunity to take them off her and into his own hands. Her eyes flirted up to meet Casey's and he didn't break his contact with her. Julia's heart sank a bit as she saw the starlight in his eyes, there was more feeling in there than he was leading on. No one looked at her that way anymore, not since she was a young woman.

She turned away, picking at the small pieces scattered by her feet. "He's right you know."

Casey gently coaxed her gaze back to his, bringing a finger to her chin. He slid his palm to the nape of her neck and caressed the side of her head with his thumb.

"I don't care. There's not much I care about these days, just my family…. and us."

This took her heart for a flight, it skipped and jumped and yearned for his touch. She leaned into his hand which pulled her closer to him. She let him pull her, let him reel her in, let him catch her. Their lips met softly at first, then passion rose in them both, swirling like a rising wild-fire. The plate was forgotten and the pieces fell to the floor again. Julia couldn't help but moan a little as Casey moved from her lips to slender neck, his tongue working wonders on her skin, just below her jaw. He pulled her up and placed her on the kitchen counter. Julia spread her legs, revealing the fruit of her womanhood and wrapped them around Casey's waist.

"Take me, Casey." She whispered into his ear like hot steam. "I'm… all yours."

Casey's blood raged with fire, her words were fuel to a furnace. With the strength of passion, he hoisted her off the counter and held her, her legs still hooked around his hips.

As they were locked in a passionate embrace, Walter marched in, ignoring them and heading directly for the water tap. "Just need some water for my pills."

Casey and Julia froze, they listened to Walter pour water into a glass and gulp it back, "Ahhhh." he exhaled, the water poultice to his thirst.

Julia eased off Casey and planted her feet back down, they stared awkwardly at one-another before Casey motioned 'Let's go.'

Under a starry night, Casey's truck pulled up to an awaiting Julia, leaning against her car. They were parked in a secluded spot overlooking the glimmering lights of the small town of Westport. Casey stepped to Julia and they reignited their fire. The couple half stumbled and tripped into Casey's truck, all the while lips joined and tongues twisting, until finally they were inside the cabin.

He pulled the door closed, Julia bit her lip as he loomed over her. Like a wild man of the sea, the primal instinct of lovemaking took him over. He ripped off his shirt and then with tender strength he lowered himself on her. His mother's dress falling like an autumn leaf. Casey ran his big hands down her thigh and their lips met once again.

Julia's breath was stolen as they became one. A low moan escaped her open mouth and her back arched up to meet his chest. She pulled his head down to hers and stared Casey right in his eyes, making sure his gaze never left hers.

"My stud." She managed through whispered moans.

He picked up the pace, in time to the waves crashing against the shore nearby. She couldn't restrain the moan that escaped her lips. They continued to stare into each other, as if together their bodies conducted an orchestra. She whirled beneath him, showing him how it was supposed to feel, being joined as one. For all her years of marriage she had stopped caring about such things, but ever since she met Casey, it was like her teens were upon her again and he was her fountain of youth. They moved through their dance, lost to themselves and distant from the rest of the world, like the stars above. Together they climbed, higher and higher as if the world were being undone and created at the same time, they both reached a true silence, like the pause between breaths, like a cresting wave about to crash. And then it did, until they both exploded. They washed upon the shore together in heavy breaths, foreheads pressed together for many moments, sharing in one breathe, without thoughts.

As they settled, he shifted to the side and she turned so that he could hold her from behind. He studied the freckles on her back like the constellations, caressing her body. It was a good while before they spoke again, the old thoughts slowly making their way into their minds once more.

"He's right. Your brother." Julia whispered.

Casey didn't speak, he let her continue, he could tell there was more to be said. He could also tell she was thinking about her husband.

"Who knew growing together meant growing apart…" Her voice trailed off for a moment. "Y'know, John was a great lover once. Now, he just pleases himself in the garage. Whenever we do 'do it', it's like he can't wait for it to be done, like it's a task to tick-off his list."

"Maybe it's hard." Casey offered. "Maybe, passion dies after a thousand fights."

Julia didn't reply but stared deep in thought, reflecting on what Casey had said. The clicking clock on the truck's dashboard came into view of her wandering eyes. Casey suddenly felt her tense up. *Here it comes.* He thought. She sat up.

"I better check on Patrick. He's camping with some of the guys from group."

"The 'Pat-signal'…" He looked away from her. "Go."

Julia felt the bitterness in his voice. He still didn't understand her position, didn't know what it was like to be a mother to a teenager, a young man only a few years younger than Casey. She stepped out of the truck and began dressing herself in her own clothes.

"Julia?"

She waited for his regular dose of guilt for leaving, but what came out of his mouth surprised her.

"Do you miss your mom?"

Julia pulled up her dress as she reflected.

"Whenever I think about her, I miss her."

She began to hook a large silver loop earring on her ear. Casey paused, taking in her answer.

"Did you feel like you lost something… When she died?" He said after a while.

"Lost?"

"Yeah. Like a feeling."

It was quiet, the wind rustled through trees, Julia adjusted her hair in the side mirror.

"You know when you lose something but you can't put your finger on it?" He continued. "Did you feel that?"

Julia thought while she folded June's dress that he had given her.

"I can't remember to be honest. It was such a long time ago."

It was obvious she was distracted. And then, because it was the right thing to do, Julia turned to Casey.

"Your mom's going to be fine."

She handed him her dress and gave a consoling look, then turned and left for her vehicle.

Casey hardly had the time to catch his breath before he heard her car spark to life and drive away. A sharp twisting pain sunk in his chest and throat, but he clenched his jaw and steeled himself against it. As he sat alone in his truck, he stared blankly at the vista before him, numb. Casey hovered between worlds, drifting further and further away from his body, the stars closer than his own beating heart.

Eventually he found himself back at home, on the back deck smoking a cigarette. He didn't know when he had got there. The world seemed more like a dream, burning slowly away, like the fuse ash of his cigarette.

In the distance the moon gleamed off the unsettled ocean, constantly moving, always in motion. Casey stared at the choppy sea, the wind became waves against the midnight sky, which came crashing down to the sandy shore. A loud wave broke and Casey was no longer there, a memory filtering out his glassy eyes.

It was a perfect day. About as perfect as you could get out at sea. There was laughter and chatter and a general mood of celebration. Douglas Treggar lifted two giant crayfish above his head, one in each arm, wielding them like trophies.

Young versions of Walter and Casey watched their father from the other side of the deck, both sporting matching 'budget' haircuts, which were slightly uneven and choppy. The sea dogs of this vessel rejoiced, congratulations as each packed their well-earned catch.

"Whatta you buying the boys, Doug?" Came an enthusiastic voice. A big toothless grin met the father in tongue and cheek.

Douglas Treggar chuckled along. "The older one; college, the young-in; a pair of balls!"

This triggered a wave of laughter from the fishermen. Casey and Walter were too young to understand the joke and they frowned at each other as if saying 'That's not funny?'

Heavy boots sounded against the deck as Captain Thomas Kyle emerged from below, holding himself with a regal authority. A son of a long line of seafarers, born and raised on the ocean, her waves as much a mother, if not more, than his own. Not two feet behind Kyle was a stone-faced man, the captain's navigator, who was never far away.

"Hell of a haul lads!" His far-set eyes wrinkled joyously, even at the age of thirty, a lifetime spent staring where the sky meets the ocean, had aged Kyle prematurely. "Treggar, your boys are our lucky rabbit's foot!"

Douglas smiled and winked at the Captain. "Walt, ova there has the feet-of a hare and gills like a damned blue-fin."

The Captain turned to Walter and took him in from head to toe.

"You free-dive, kid?" The Captain said in a voice you could not ignore, addressing Walter directly.

Walter froze like a dear in the headlights, he was not used to being addressed by such a character. All eyes turned to him which made him freeze even more. The Captain offered the kid a light smile, and like a drifting breeze turned his eyes back to Douglas.

"You bet he does. Tell 'em your time Walt!" The proud father responded.

"Umm. Two minutes thirty. Sir. Maybe three. Sir."

The crew laughed at the child's formality.

The Captain was thoroughly impressed, raising one eyebrow inquisitively, a wry smile forming. "You gotta good kid there, Doug."

Like developing film exposed to light too soon, the memory bled away and Casey found himself back on the deck of his mother's home. His cigarette had burned down, and he dropped it carelessly to the wooden panels below.

Casey made his way back to his room, a drifting bird with no island to land on. He didn't know what time he finally fell asleep, nor did he feel rested when he awoke. His eyes were red and stinging, his heart heavy and dulled. He lay in bed for a long while. He could hear Walter moving about outside. The morning birds sung their songs then ceased, and the sun which was low in the sky, got higher and higher.

~

June was still asleep on her hospital bed. Casey sat by her side. He was as distant as ever, staring off into nothing, holding her limp frail hand. Walter stood in his usual spot by the window, far away in the world outside, distant like his brother. At some point Casey snapped out of his daze and looked over to Walter. He quietly watched him, and Walter's reflection in the clear window. A scowl began to form. He shouldn't have to ask him again, in that moment Casey despised his brother. How could he sit there so cold, so removed? Did he even care? After everything that Casey and his mother had done for him, this was his thanks. Casey let out a dismissive sigh through clenched teeth and shook his head before turning back to June.

Her mouth was ajar and dry. The whites of her eyes could be seen rolled-up in her head, her eyelids not reaching all the way closed. Casey's anger switched to sadness once more.

"Hey Mom. It's Casey."

He waited for a reaction.

None came.

"Walter's here as well."

Silence.

"We tried that recipe you got for us a couple days back. It was okay, but nothing like you would have made."

Casey closed his eyes. Waiting. Hoping for a response. Anything, even just a single sound. June's silence was a ghost about the room that haunted the place between words. Casey couldn't feel her anywhere. It was the most disconcerting feeling to have his mother right there in front of him, yet not have her there at all. It was as if this body that he had associated with her, since the moment he was born, was but a hollow shell. June existed somewhere else, and she was buried deep. What was she picturing right now, what was she experiencing? Was it all dark and empty and nothingness? Or was she dreaming? Was she hovering above them right now in the room, trying to be heard.

Casey listened deeper, strained his mind and ears.

Silence.

Silence amidst the beeping hospital machines.

"Walter is much better now. He's living with us at home, back in his old room."

Casey was trying to pull her out of her slumber with good news, giving her spirit a reason to live. Walter from the window shifted his gaze at the mention of his name and watched his brother's attempt at communication.

"We went to see Father O'Brien yesterday." Casey continued.

They hadn't. But Walter understood what Casey was trying to do.

"He said a prayer for you. We all said a prayer. You see. Now God has to make you better. He knows you've got people down here who need you."

June was a spiritual woman. She always pulled the boys to church on Sundays, dressing-up in their finest shirts and trousers. Making sure their hair was combed and they were presentable to the congregation.

Walter couldn't help but feel a swelling of emotions as he watched his brother.

"Please." Casey prayed, more to some higher power than to his mother. "Please wake up."

June lay still, unresponsive. Walter watched. He watched Casey hide his face and wipe away loose tears with a trembling hand. He watched his brother quietly cry to himself, hunched over the near corpse of their mother.

Casey only let the tears stream for a few moments before he pulled himself together. The wind howled outside and the trees strained against their roots, gentle sprays of sea carried in ocean breeze. Casey straightened himself and looked at Walter from over his chair, his brother met his gaze for a moment, but a strong pluck of guilt quickly interrupted him and his eyes darted away in shame. Unable to stare at the face of his grieving brother.

The rest of the day was grey. Even though the wild winds blew the clouds away, they sky was bright for many and children played in the harbor, running along the floating wooden docks. Kites flew in the large open fields, swirling colors of the rainbow and some even shaped like dragons. But for Walter, it remained a daze, even the brilliant weather left him unfazed. Nothing it seems could pull him out of the place he was trapped, where he lived most days. Casey today joined him, the laughter around them passing like silt. It was one of those days where the joy of others didn't serve to uplift but rather as a form to irritate.

The day was short for both brothers. And the setting sun was a relief, darkness it seemed was the setting they were waiting for.

Walter turned the tap for the bath. Scalding water came rushing out, steaming in swirls around the brightly tiled bathroom. He slowly turned the knob for cold, letting it add gradually until it reached a desired temperature. He watched it fill up, watched the water circulate. In what seemed like the length of a blink, the bathtub was almost full. Slightly surprised, he quickly turned off the faucet.

The warm water soothed him instantly as Walter slipped his body in deeper and deeper. Eventually his ears were submerged and the only sound was that of his heart, beating the blood through his veins.

"Walter!"

Came the echoing voice of his father, Douglas Treggar.

The voice pulled Walter deep into the memory.

The Majestic was anchored in place and the Treggar family, minus June, were huddled together by the edge of the deck.

"It's not safe." Douglas cautioned, whispering in Walter's ear.

Captain Kyle walked up with his heavy boots and sailor grin.

"What's the story fellas? The blue hole awaits."

All the crew and deck-hands were gathered around, waiting in anticipation, excited for the show. The Majestic floated beside a deep blue hole that seemed to extend forever into the ocean's heart, its' depths lost to the seeing eye. The *blue hole* as it was called, was a giant gape in the reef that extended for miles beneath the surface. Many free divers would come to test themselves in its inviting depths, some never to return.

Douglas stood from his kneel besides Walter.

"Casey. Take your brother below deck, and wait for me there."

The crew looked impatient, it appeared as if they had gathered for nothing.

"Let's go…" One of the deck hands ushered to a nearby crew member.

"The kid's scared, Cap."

They were about to disassemble when the Captain decided to try one last effort to get the kid to dive.

"How about, if you bring me back a souvenir son; I double your pop's share!"

Walter perked at this idea. He was confident and all the watching eyes made him want to prove himself even more, especially with his father present to witness the achievement. He would come back a hero and his dad would get a huge reward. This was something Walter wasn't going to pass up. He had dived at similar depths but not this far from shore and into the abyss of a blue-hole.

Douglas on the other hand was not too comfortable with the idea of his son free-diving into an uncharted expanse in the ocean. He was shaking his head in the direction of the Captain with a dismissive smile, but was interrupted by a small hand tugging on his shirt. Walter was star-ing up at his father with determined eyes.

"I can do it, dad."

This took Douglas by surprise. He wasn't used to Walter being so ready to take on a challenge.

"See, Doug. The kid has spoken." Chuckled Captain Kyle.

Douglas kneeled back down on the deck, so that he was eye-level with his sons.

"Are you sure about this Walt? You don't need to prove anything to me or anyone aboard. It could be dangerous down there."

Walter stared his dad in the eyes. "I can do this."

Douglas gave his son a solid pat on the shoulder. "Well…. Then, go get 'em!'"

Walter beamed from ear-to-ear at his father's encouragement.

The crew cheered!

"You got this Walt!"

"Give the Captain a show for his money!"

Walter took the applause and took-off his shirt. With practiced calm, he walked to the edge of the ship. He could feel his heart beating wildly but he steadied himself with deep breaths, just like he was taught.

3, 2, 1. Splash!

He dove into the clear waters, and another wave of cheers ensued. Casey clicked on his stopwatch and the timer began its count.

The shock of ice-cold water hit Walter's body as he entered the ocean, his dive was streamlined and hardly a splash was made as he rocketed down. Like a swordfish he cut through the water, and the cold only served to jolt his adrenaline, giving him strength. Once the momentum of his dive came to a halt he began to swim, scooping the water around him with his palms and kicking in rhythm. The cavernous opening was daunting, like a gigantic sea creature's mouth, threatening to swallow him whole. But, Walter just kept swimming, pushing past the fear of the giant cave below him. This was for his dad, for his brother, his mom and the entire Treggar family. Now, they would all be proud of him, were the kinds of whispers his ego fed off to propel his drive.

The surface got further and further away, and so did the light become less. Walter stared into an endless blue, for that was all that lived here, beneath the scattered rays of the sun. Deeper and deeper he forged, and soon his lungs began to burn. It was much harder than when he practiced with his father. Here there was no rope to help pull him up. He didn't have a clip for his nose, and a lot of his energy was lost to the nervous excitement that sent him catapulting down in the first place. The bottom was still a way away, but it was too late to turn back now.

He spared no glance back towards the surface and pushed his little body deeper and deeper. He could hear his heart in his ears and every part of his body was screaming at him to breathe, screaming at him to take a fresh gulp of air. That was impossible here. All that would do is fill his lungs with sea water. The only thought in his head was a plead to turn around, to return to the surface, but Walter kept struggling against his mind, battling on and on.

When he thought he couldn't move one more muscle he reached the entrance. The tips of his fingers touched the reef floor.

"Walter!" It was Casey's voice this time.

~

"Walter!"

His limp body was pulled out of the water and into Douglas's arms. He cradled his lifeless child, panic and bottomless dread in the father's heart. As fast as he could and with as much care possible in such situations, Douglas lay Walter on the deck and immediately commenced trying to revive his son. He pinched the child's nose and breathed his own air into Walter, as if giving him his own life. Everyone stood around the father and son speechless, hands covering their mouths, praying that this not be the day the ocean takes another soul.

Douglas was pressing the water out of Walter's lungs with his large fatherly hands, and Casey turned his brother's head to the side so that the water could flow-out with ease.

The navigator ran to the command station and the familiar static of the CB-Radio could be heard as he alerted the authorities, requesting an ambulance at their arrival.

Walter stood there now. As an adult. Witnessing the tragedy as it happened. The day his whole life crumbled to pieces. He watched the childhood fragment of himself laying there unconscious and still, whilst the world fought to revive him.

From the back of his mind June's voice cut in through the chaos.

"Walt. Sweetie. Wake up."

Douglas and Casey pushed every ounce of life into Walter that they could, their desperation rising. There was a flicker of movement in Walter's eyes and then… Coughing.

Walter was coughing. Heaving seawater from the depths of his lungs. Douglas faltered back, falling onto his rear in disbelief and haze. He was alive. His son was alive. Casey lifted his brothers head and cradled it in his lap, crying from joy.

With the little consciousness that Walter had left, he placed a smooth stone into his father's hand. Douglas took it in. Walter had done it. He made it to the reef. Douglas was shocked and not sure how to act, he just continued to stare at his son as Walter drifted in and out of consciousness, the stone gripped firmly in his right hand. Douglas didn't even notice the ship moving towards the harbor, or the flashing ambulance lights by the docks.

Meanwhile, the adult Walter watched the scene unfold, a third-party observer to his own tragedy. They were nearing the docks when the scene was interrupted by an omniscient voice. It cascaded down from the sky, the voice of his mother.

"Walt. Can you hear me?"

Walter turned to see where the voice landed.

All of a sudden, he was with her. His mom. Except they were no longer on the boat. They were in a hospital room, and June was younger, vibrant and alive. Her skin showed no signs of age, as of yet.

"Can you hear me?" She whispered again.

The sight of his mother in front of him was like warm honey melting. Immediately the young Walter began to tear.

"Mom… I'm sorry."

She smiled in her motherly way.

"No one's mad at you, honey. We're all just happy you're okay."

Something gnawed at Walter's attention, and when he followed the blur of voices behind his mother's head, he saw Casey and his dad outside the window of the hospital room, standing in the hall observing. There were police officers present as well. He could barely just make out what they were saying.

"You're a hero kid. If it wasn't for you, your brother would be at the bottom of the ocean."

Casey took in the officer's words with pride and strength. However, Douglas on the other hand was staring directly at Walt through the thick glass, guilt burdened his every pore. This had happened on his watch, he should never have let Walter dive.

The look in his father's eyes and the coaxing voice of June's voice were the last things Walter remembered, as the sounds of his heart brought him back to the present. The water had cooled to a mild warm, tepid temperature, and he could feel the prune on his fingers. Slowly, very slowly, he got out of the bathtub.

~

Casey stepped from his room into the darkly lit corridor of their family home. He couldn't help but glance at Walter's empty bedroom as he passed it. With a heavy heart he approached his mother's chambers and opened the door with a somber creak. The lights were off, yet the moon shone rays through the open window, illuminating pockets of space and casting dancing shadows across the room. A tiny red light was glowing in one of the pockets of shadow. As Casey's eyes adjusted, the silhouette of a grown man became apparent. It was Walter.

He was leaning against the far wall, smoking. Casey could just make out the contours of his face, and just as he could Walter smiled. Casey relaxed, a weight slipped-off him as he smiled back.

"Can't sleep." Walter stated.

Casey smiled again and nodded. Him neither.

Walter's eyes wandered around the room.

Casey observed him for a moment, before he asked "What you looking for?"

"Nothing. I'm just taking in the small things. The pieces that made mom."

Casey nodded in approval and began to do the same. He took in all the little things that reflected June. A fine brush, with a small amount of hair tangled in its comb. An open jewelry box, there was no worry that anything to be stolen. Well used shoes tucked neatly beside the bed. A picture of Walter and Casey in their school uniforms, arms around one another and smiling huge grins.

"What are you going to do with all of her things?" Walter asked.

Casey leaned against the wall by the door, there was a pause as he thought to himself.

"I don't know. Give it to charity. Not sure where half that jewelry came from. Mom liked mail order, I guess."

"I'd like to keep some." Walt said. A tone of tenderness carried in his voice that Casey hadn't heard in a long time.

"You can have all her dresses and make-up, happy?" Casey teased.

"I think your girlfriend will want those."

Casey wasn't amused but he let the joke slide.

"Why don't you say anything to mom?"

There was no response.

"Walt?"

Walter sighted. "I don't know what to say."

"Tell her that you love her, that you miss her."

"She knows all that Casey."

Casey was about to retort when something inside him paused. Walter was right. She did know all those things. Did Casey talk to his mother for her recovery, or did he talk to her for himself, for his own sanity? So that he could feel better. So that he didn't have to sit with her silence and share the emptiness she was enduring.

Walter interrupted his thoughts.

"Why did you lie to her? We never saw Father O'Brian. No one prayed for her."

Casey slid down the wall he was leaning against and came to sit on the floor.

"I just want her to get better." He said.

"Casey. We both know she's going to die. We have to face it. Don't lie to her like that."

"I wouldn't have to if you said anything!" Casey replied defensively.

He waited for Walter to put him in his place, but no voice sounded from the shadows. Just deep breaths and the quiet crackle of cigarette fire.

"By the way, I warned you already, Walt. Don't smoke inside this house."

Casey picked himself up and strode back to his room. Walter on the other hand extinguished his finished cigarette in between his thumb and forefinger, then struck up a fresh one in defiance. All the while staring towards the empty door where Casey had left through.

CHAPTER SIX

The next morning was like any other workday. Casey found himself walking through the ugly Southern Marine plant wishing he didn't have to be there. Workers filed in beside him, most likely sharing the same feeling. Another monotonous day in paradise. His mind was blank and the legs of his body moved him like clockwork. Just another will bent to work for an intolerable machine. Gene, the machine's herald, stood watch at the entrance, his eyes hawk-like sharp. Casey nodded 'good morning' in his direction out of necessary politeness, and not because he desired.

Gene smiled approvingly, tapping on his watch. *On time.*

Great… Casey mirrored his sentiment, with well-masked contempt.

~

Through the window of an arts room, a group of teenagers ran around amongst one another, throwing and kicking balls around. The movement of their bodies reminded Walter of how the leaves scatter on windy days. He found himself wishing he could join them. Instead he was stuck inside.

A small, caged barrel full of numbered balls rattled around tirelessly He was stuck inside with the patients deemed unfit to play with the rest of the teenagers. The Bingo host called out numbers in an overly enthusiastic voice, trying to generate some excitement in an otherwise completely tired game.

"One, one, legs eleven!" The Rec. Worker cried out.

A few people marked their scorecards, some seemed too lost to follow what was going on.

A teenager leaned over and asked Walter a question. He had never bothered to learn any of their names, nor did he have any intention of doing so.

"What did she say? Legs?"

"Eleven." Walter filled in the gaps. "She's an idiot, buddy."

"I said, 11!" The woman enunciated even louder, which made Walter wince. "And, I'm not an idiot. Just trying to make this fun."

Walter apologized to her with a shrug, whilst the person next to him marked eleven on his card.

She ignored him. "Two, four, lock your door. Twenty four!"

God. She's such an idiot. Walter thought, to himself this time, smiling.

The kids next to him turned to Walter for support once again.

"Twenty four." Walter mumbled, crossing his arms.

"Eight, eight. We can all be great! Eighty eight!"

Walter cringed inside. He'd had enough.

"Hey! Do I need permission to… take a leak?"

"Yes. But go ahead, and hurry back! We've got singing next!" The support worker half-sung the response.

Walter couldn't get out of there sooner. Relief washed over him as he finally left that lady and her annoying voice behind, not to mention the drone of those rattling balls.

He found that he had actually needed to use the restroom. When he stepped out, wiping his hands on a paper towel, he could hear an orchestra of off-key singing meandering its way from up the hall.

"Hell no." Walter grunted to himself. He searched for somewhere to discard the paper-towel, just then he spotted a bin across the hallway, it was far but Walter was up for the challenge. He scrunched a paper ball and went for the half-court buzzer beater. The ball flew across the room and appeared to be aimed well, it was going in… but caught the edge, bounced-off and landed on the ground.

Before he proceeded to dispose it, Walter did a quick survey of the hall, it was empty. Good. Just past the room of murderous singing there was a door marked 'exit'. Trying to appear as nonchalant as possible Walter dared his escape. He slipped past the arts room, collected his ball, backhanded it into the bin *'Swish!'* and stepped out into the fresh air. Just as he was about to inhale a deep victorious breath, a voice interrupted him from nearby.

"Where are you going?"

It was Patrick.

Walter snapped around, stunned and caught like a fish out of water. However, his alarm was misguided. From the glint in Patrick's eyes, Walter could tell that he was making a run for it as well. Walter let himself relax.

"I'm going fishing."

Patrick raised his eyebrows. "Is it any fun? Can you… teach me?"

Pleasantly surprised by the kid's response, Walter smiled and motioned with his head for the kid to follow.

It began to rain as they set off, but Walter was undeterred and trudged along equally determined. Patrick lifted his light denim jacket above his head to protect his hair. Walter quickly walked around the building and headed straight for the road, with Patrick following close behind.

~

Meanwhile at the plant Casey was marking notes on a clipboard, with Julia loading packed products onto a weighing machine. There was the sound of the office phone ringing in the distance. It disappeared into the background noise of the plant, and Casey hardly paid it any notice to it. That was until he heard his name being called.

"Casey, it's for you!" One of the workers called out.

Casey shook his head. "I'm busy, Todd."

"It's Gene. Something about your brother."

"Ah crap." Casey mumbled under his breath. What now.

Just then Julia's phone beeped. What was she doing with that? Workers were meant to leave them in the lockers. She did not look happy. She strode the distance between them and shoved her phone in Casey's face A message on the screen read 'Patrick is missing."

Panic and dread set into Casey.

"Find them, before I tell John."

Julia took the clipboard out of his hand.

Dammit. Casey quickly nodded thanks in her direction before jogging towards management.

Casey arrived in Genes office while he was engaged on the phone. Gene put his hand over the receiver, so whoever it was on the other line couldn't hear what he was about to say.

"Your brother ran-off from his program."

Casey had already assumed as much. He tried to contain his frustration. Gene returned to his call but Casey remained in the doorway. After a couple moments Gene noticed he was still standing there. He gave Casey a disapproving look and motioned him away with his hands, like a fly.

"I'm really sorry. It won't happen again." Casey apologized.

"Well, we've all got our priorities. I'll get Roger down to cover." Gene returned his attention to the phone. "Sorry, I'll have to call you back." He then preceded to dial another number.

"Thanks Gene."

Gene didn't reply and continued his call.

Casey ran out, fumbling to pull his car keys out of his pocket. He tried to think of where Walter would go. Town center wasn't far away, he would start there.

Casey slowly drove down every main road, making sure to peer into restaurants and shops as he passed them. But had no luck.

Then, realization dawned on him all of a sudden.

"Of course!"

He u-turned the truck immediately and sped off towards the pier.

Walter was fishing at the edge of a rocky stretch of land with branches linked with fishing line. It jutted out from the main beach, and many fathers went there to catch small fish with their kids. Walter was teaching Patrick the basics, how to cast a line and where to aim it.

A strong wind blew in their direction, away from the city.

Casey pulled up at the beach and could see two figures in the distance. He jumped out of the truck and ran towards them.

"Walter!" Casey yelled as he stormed up.

Walter ignored him, keeping his focus on his line. He knew the kill joys from the program were bound to call Casey at one point or another. As he got closer, Casey recognized that the person beside him was Patrick, he had held out hope that the two wouldn't be together. The magnitude of the situation dawned on him. Jesus. An adult man taking a minor from a corrective program to a secluded beach. This was not going to look good.

"What the hell, Walt?!"

"What." Walter said through gritted teeth, annoyed that he couldn't steal even a couple moments of free-time for himself.

"What do you mean what? They've called the cops!"

"That's…. crazy. I was gonna go back."

"I asked you not to get in anymore trouble. You couldn't even last a week without screwing it up."

Patrick's eyes darted between the brothers as they spoke, unsure of what stance to take.

"Patrick. Toss the line. Please. Wait by my truck."

He shrugged and dropped the stick by his feet. Just as he did so, something tugged at the line and the stick was yanked into the ocean.

"Aww man…" Patrick grieved. "Damn it. All this waiting for nothing." He looked genuinely disappointed.

"It's okay, buddy. Better luck next time." Walter assured.

They both looked genuinely crushed.

"There won't be a next time!" Casey yelled. "Patrick. Truck."

The teenager gave Walter a look of solidarity before shoving his hands in his pockets and trudging towards the truck, stepping from rock to rock with his long legs.

"I'm sorry." Walter said, as Patrick cleared the rocks and landed on the beach outside of earshot.

"Dammit Walt! I don't care if you're sorry. He is a minor!"

Walter stared at Casey blankly, they were just having innocent fun.

"Yeah." Walter replied sheepishly.

"You could get in a lot of trouble for this."

Walter didn't reply.

"Come on, let's go."

Walter followed behind with his head down.

"You know you're going to get me fired. You do know that right?!" Casey ranted, shaking his head. "They're definitely taking you back now, Walt."

Just then Casey's phone rang. The wind blew both brother's hair in wild patterns as they traversed the rocks back to shore. The caller ID read Julia's name. For a moment Casey thought of not answering the phone but decided against that, after all she was a worried parent, regardless of their relationship.

"Hey. Yes. Pat's fine. Yeah. I'm taking them back now."

Julia sighed in relief.

Walter couldn't hear what was being said on her side, there was a long awkward pause in the conversation.

"Julia? Hello?"

The line cut off. She had hung up on Casey.

CHAPTER SEVEN

———— ◆ ◇ ◆ ————

By the time it took Casey to drop Patrick off and arrive in the Psychiatric Hospital lounge, it was already ten past five. He had missed another day of work. The old Seiko wall-clock was silent as it ticked. Casey hovered by it impatiently, waiting for the staff to call him. Walter sat on the other side of the room, slumped into one of the faux leather couches. There were other patients around him staring blankly at a television screen, drawn to some reality-show on about a man and his dog, as if in a hypnotic trance. There was a member of hospital staff seated next to Walter, but truth be told she was more interested in the show that anyone else. Maybe she was the one who had switched channels. Everyone, Casey observed was more interested in escaping the moment of time they were currently in, than being present to savor it.

Walter snuck a glance at Casey, trying to judge how mad he was. Casey felt Walter's eyes on him and sternly shook his head, eyes furious. *Not good.* Walter thought.

The soft sound of footsteps approached. A kind middle aged lady who seemed like she had seen too much misery for her years, emerged from an open doorway at the end of the main corridor.

"Casey." Her name tag read HEATHER in all capital letters. "Thanks for waiting. We're ready for you."

Casey nodded. He shot Walter a paternal glare before walking off towards her and disappearing into the room.

The room was rather sparse. There was a single rectangular table in the center, with three people seated behind it. There was Heather, Walter's assigned social worker, Dr. Wallace and the program director Nancy. Casey took his place opposite them, sitting in an uncomfortable plastic chair. He was definitely on edge, watching the three people in front of him sort through papers and files, quietly whispering to one another, strengthening their position. Finally, Heather looked up and addressed Casey directly. She got straight to the point.

"As you know Casey, we've been quite lenient with your brother. Due to his condition and a series of repeated incidents, we have no other choice but to recommend that he be housed in a secure, supervised facility."

"Okay." Casey said, trying to make eye contact with the other two people at the table, but they were busy looking through papers.

"He needs the attention that his institution in Seattle can provide." Heather went on.

"Are you saying what I think you're saying?"

Heather took off her glasses so she could stare at him, eye-to-eye. There was genuine sincerity to the way she looked at him.

"I'm sorry Casey. But it appears, Walter requires the discipline and attention that only an institution can provide. That's our formal opinion in this matter."

While Casey appreciated her sentiment, there was no way he was going to let that happen without a fight.

"You don't understand, I have to keep him *here*. It's my mother's wish." He didn't have the strength to extrapolate his last statement further. "What's the worst case?"

The trio behind the desk exchanged weary glances before Heather turned back towards him.

"Well, the closest facility that could properly monitor him is Washington Correctional's Psyche Wing, it's not too far from here."

Casey scowled in disbelief. He couldn't believe what he was hearing.

"Are you kidding?! That's a prison! You can't send him there."

Heather gave him a look that said 'what else are we meant to do?' and the rest of the Board looked uncomfortable.

"No. He is not going there. There has to be something else, we have to find another way."

Casey made it very clear. The Board deliberated for a couple moments, whispering to themselves from behind their desk. Heather looked-up once they were done.

"Look, why don't I call you in the next few days and let you know where things stand? Are you able to take care of Walter until then?"

Casey nodded. He had no other choice it appeared.

"Dr. Wallace, Nancy." She turned to the people sitting either side of her. "Do you have anything to add?"

Nancy was the first to speak.

"Just that you should keep working with him on the actives Dr. McKenzie recommended."

Casey nodded politely.

"And continue to monitor his reaction to the medication." Dr Wallace added. "I think you will start to see some improvements, as long as there's *impetus,* something to jolt his memory."

Again, Casey nodded, he reflected on Dr. Wallace's words.

"These are copies of his medical information." Heather motioned a folder and paper bag.

Nancy got up from the table and walked over towards him, bag and folder in hand. Casey took the items from her.

"Call us if you have any problems." Dr. Wallace assured, already glimpsing over another patient's file.

"Sure."

The room went quiet, it was obvious they had reached a stalemate, and regardless, Casey had nothing left to say. Heather offered him a sympathetic smile. Casey left them without another word.

~

Casey and Walter sat in silence as they drove away from the hospital. Walter stared out the window, wondering if this was the last time he would see Westport.

"Are you taking me back?" Walter finally asked.

Casey didn't reply immediately, he wanted Walter to think about how close he has come to getting shipped off.

"No."

"Then where are we going?"

"To see mom."

Walter was extremely relieved. He hadn't realized how much he liked being back, how much he enjoyed being away from that place until now. He nodded slowly, thanking Casey with his silence.

"Are you mad?" He asked.

Casey didn't reply, and Walter could see by his brother's expression and tight grip on the wheel that he was.

"As long as you're not mad." Walter mumbled.

Casey kept his gaze focused on the road, but shifted in his seat sporadically, trying to contain his frustration.

Eventually they arrived at June's hospital. The familiar sterile scent of cleaning products and sick people greeted them as they headed to their mother's room. June's vital monitors beeped away, she was still asleep, nothing new. Casey resumed his usual spot by his mother's side, and Walter made his way to the window, but not without sparing a quick glance in his mother's direction. Casey wasn't having it today, not today.

"Walt. You sit here." He demanded.

Walter pleaded his resignation but Casey was dead serious. He wasn't getting out of this one. Reluctantly, Walter shuffled towards the bed, sitting as far away from Casey as possible. He intentionally avoided eye contact with both of them, whilst Casey reached forward and caressed June's hand.

"Mom, Walter's here. He wants to say goodbye."

Walter looked up from his seat confused. 'What do you mean *goodbye.*' He seemed to say. But, Casey paid him no heed.

"Say goodbye, Walt."

Walter didn't reply immediately, trying to gage Casey's expression, but his brother would not make eye contact with him.

"Why are you doing this?"

"Just say goodbye." Casey replied firmly.

"Look, Case."

"No, you look! You've been hiding behind what happened out there all these years. If you did it to get out of work, not face responsibilities. Then fine. I don't care."

Walter was evidently taken back and offended.

"Mom is running out of time, Walt. And, I've run out of patience."

Walter was lost for words. He glanced between his mother and Casey, trying to muster up a few syllables, but everything fell short.

"What do you remember about that day, the day you drowned?" Casey said softly.

"You know what happened, you were there."

"Tell me again."

"Casey…"

"Tell me again!"

"I was diving, trying to beat my time. I… passed out at the bottom. Then you dove in after me. I woke up, saw you and dad. That's it."

"Lies, Walter." Casey tried to contain his anger but it still came out. "I know that's not all you remember!"

Walter looked confused. He had recounted this moment over and over again for the past twenty years, there was nothing more add, the record had dulled and the music had distorted into a static hum. What was Casey trying to extract from him?

"I'm sorry if I don't remember your big moment, Casey." Walter turned to his mother. "Bye mom."

Then, Walter got up and stormed off.

Stunned Casey watched as his brother simply walked away.

"Don't you walk away from us! Sit down, Walt!"

Just as he reached the border of the door to the hallway, Walter turned around.

"Who said you could play dad? Huh, Casey? I'm your *older* brother!"

Casey immediately rose from his chair, leaving June's hand behind on the bed.

"He left us, you jerk! I had to play dad! Why didn't *you* leave school, all your wild dreams and gut fish, huh!?"

Walter shook his head, his face scrunching into anger. He looked at Casey as if he was about to spit on him, then turned and stormed away.

"Go on. Runaway Walt." Casey followed him, yelling at his back. "When things get tough, you do what you do best."

Walter kept walking. Casey glimpsed his own face in the reflection of one of the patient windows and stopped in his tracks. *Dammit.* All of a sudden, he regretted every word that had left his mouth.

"Wait. Walter!"

But Walter didn't stick around, there was no point, if Casey was going to be condescending and abusive, he let him be so on his own. Sure, Walter had his problems, but he wasn't some child that could be yelled at and treated with disdain. Walter was more intuitive than he led-on, but people only saw the outside, the fact he was mentally ill. That one stigma labelled Walter as something below normal and gave the labeler a deluded sense of reign over him. Whether people were implicit or not, it was an unavoidable degradation of him and of his self-worth. There had been very few who looked at him as he truly was and not some mentally-ill shipwreck. Even Casey, his own brother treated him like an inconvenience, like an annoying itch. To hell with them all. Walter didn't turn back once as he left Casey, red and heated. Even as Casey yelled his name, Walter ignored it.

Casey's eyes were fixed on where Walter had disappeared from view, and they remained there for a long while after he was gone. Casey hated how easily his own temper got away from him, if only he had taken a couple breaths and really thought about things, before he spoke in anger. Because, every time he regretted everything he had said. Casey and Walter were past apologies now, sometimes sorry is a hollow shell for someone who is never going to change. Sorry is said to try and make things better, it's words without actions, and Casey knew that only actions would speak to his brother now.

After a long while, Casey finally turned away. June's nurse was watching from her station. No words were exchanged between the two of them. There was nothing to say. With his hands in his pockets, Casey slowly walked back to his mother's room, closing the door gently behind him.

~

That evening, Walter sat by himself amongst other worshipers, on the hard wooden bench of the local church. Father O'Brian's hands came together, his fingers interlocking in deep prayer. The Father stood starkly behind his podium, Jesus open on the crucifix hung down from the ceiling behind him, casting shadows onto the priest's stage. Beside Walter, a woman who looked as if she carried ten worlds upon her shoulders, was kneeling and praying feverishly. Tears streamed down her cheeks and both her eyes and hands were squeezed tight.

Walter watched her and after a moment decided to follow her in prayer. He humbled himself and knelt before the alter of Jesus Christ. Slowly his palms came together and with all the pain he had inside, Walter squeezed his hands into a pleading prayer, hoping to awake his savior. For the first time in his life, he truly reached out to God. Walter dropped his shield of irony and opened-up to the possibility of something grander than himself. He prayed in vigil until the last candle was blown out.

~

Casey was still in his mother's room, the hours merged into a timeless absence. He stared into nothing, his hand still lightly pressed against June's. He couldn't let go. Not yet. It was too soon. He wasn't ready to lose his mother. The closeness of her death weighed upon his chest, and no part of him could not handle the feeling. He stood outside his body, as if he was watching himself from a third person's point of view. He watched himself hold June's hand. Removed from the situation, removed from any feeling in his heart. He couldn't face what everyone knew was coming. So, he hung in a limbo, dissociated from the world. The only anchor back to reality was his mother's cold hand inside of his own. Casey thought how easy it would be to get lost and just remove himself from life.

The woman he loved was married. Julia sat with him now, her husband, on the couch in her home, cuddled with their son, and warm by the television. Julia held Patrick's hand, and squeezed it gently.

Casey was nothing more than a playful distraction, something to keep her entertained.

Wild thoughts raced madly in his mind.

His brother resented him, and with good reason. He'd kept him locked away like some monstrosity, in a mental facility hundreds of miles away. What kind of brother did that?

And his mom. She was half a breath away from death. The only good thing in his life was a meagre promotion, at a job he hated. Why had he worked so hard? For what? Casey's whole life began crumbling to pieces before him.

Walter sat alone on the fisherman's rocky stretch. The ocean wind gently blew his hair, the ocean spray speckled across his face. Walter sat facing the vast ocean before him, dark and endless. In the distance, just before the horizon break, lightning struck. The bright scar across the sky left its imprint on Walter's retina as he closed his eyes. A blue streak of fire hovered in the dark.

CHAPTER EIGHT

◆◇◆

Casey made it home and collapsed on his bed after spending most of the night in his mother's room. The nurse had let him sleep on the visitor's chairs.

It was morning. Upon waking, Casey found Walter sleeping on the front porch. He had left the door unlocked, yet still Walter had decided to pass out on the wooden deck. He let Walter sleep a bit longer, he wasn't ready to be in company yet.

Casey's phone rang. The caller ID revealed a name that sent spikes of anxiety through him. Life would be easier if he never had to see that man again.

"Hello."

Immediately the voice on the other side of the line began to speak in a raised voice. Casey just listened, only half in his body. Gene's lecture felt distant and Casey sat patiently waiting for him to finish his tirade. his thoughts traveled to Walter, to his mother, and of course to Julia.

"Do you understand me Casey!" Gene yelled, hurting Casey's ear with the sheer volume of sound.

"Yes. I understand." Casey responded. The inflection in his voice numb and muted.

Gene went on again. Casey let Gene's words merge into a stream of meaningless sounds. Meanwhile, Casey glanced out the window. The day was grey and overcast but the birds still sang. The diffused light through the clouds shone through the windows and onto the floor of the Treggar's living room floor.

"Yes, ofcourse the position means a lot to me…" Casey lied, but was cut off before he could finish.

The lecture continued.

"I'll sort it out, Gene. Once an' for all"

They hung up without saying so much as a goodbye, both were now at the end of their tether.

Casey knew that one more slip-up and Gene would have no other option but to fire him, his own credibility was on the line. Maybe that wouldn't be as bad as he imagined, since his brother's arrival Casey had glimpsed his life and saw that it was nothing more than a series of have-to's, with responsibility increasing gradually. The temperature had slowly risen and now, it was boiling. Amidst the birds Walter's snoring carried on into the house and brought Casey out of his thoughts, it was time to wake him up.

Casey opened the door and stood over him, watching as his brother slept deeply, mouth agape and drooling onto the front porch. Casey nudged Walter with his foot a couple times and with a sudden breath Walter came to, looking around as if he didn't remember where he was. Then through squinted eyes he stared up at Casey who was holding a cup of morning coffee for him.

Walter groaned and retreated a bit, unsure of what Casey was going to say.

"Get dressed Walt."

Walter nodded, as he took the cup from Casey. At last the ball had dropped. He was going back to the looney bin. But, instead Casey announced, "We're going fishing."

The words took Walter by surprise, they sounded about as real as an angel appearing before him, perhaps he was still dreaming and misheard.

"Wait, what? Really?"

"Go on. Grab your stuff."

Walter used one of the porch chairs to help himself stand. He took another look at Casey and made sure he was serious. His brother just raised an eye-brow in expectation. Still surprised and rather pleased, Walter hurried into the house to get ready.

It was only fifteen minutes before they were on the move, driving east on the main road. The short clips of songs and radio waves shifted as Walter rejected several radio stations trying to find something to suit the mood.

"Just pick something." Casey twitched, irritated by the switching.

"I wish I could. It's either ancient or an ad, even the songs."

"Then, let's just talk."

Walter switched off the radio. In the silence that ensued neither could find the words to instigate a conversation. Walter sat awkwardly fumbling with his fingers. Casey noticed and rolled his eyes.

"Y'know, there was something that I was meaning to ask." Casey said breaking the silence. "When was the last time you had sex?"

The question took Walter off-guard with it's bluntness, he blushed and shied away, deciding whether or not to answer. Then the mischievous boy in him came forward and he had to hide his smile as he replied.

"This nurse, back in Seattle."

"No way. Really? A nurse. Walt, you Casanova."

"She was friendly."

"I bet."

The brothers exchanged wry smiles.

Casey continued the banter. "She probably had a lot of practice too. It's a big hospital."

But Walter, didn't throw anything back, instead got defensive. "She wasn't like that, Casey. She told me I was different. That I was the first patient she'd, you know…"

"Relieved of their ailment?"

Walter lightly shook his head, smiling. Taking the jab from his brother.

"Did this really happen, Walt?" Casey jested, narrowing his eyes.

"I'm not lying. She was real."

"Alright, alright." Casey said, easing out the tension. "I'm not saying she wasn't. What was her name?"

"Debra. From Dallas." Walter casually muttered.

"Debbie… From Dallas…" Casey's jaw dropped, was his brother kidding. He looked over and saw his brother smiling. "Ha, very funny, Walt."
Walter sat smugly, looking rather pleased with himself.

"Alright, enough. You hungry?"

"Yeah, sure." Walter replied, feeling in good spirits.

Casey turned the truck, pulling into a rest stop. One of those places that sells everything. The paint on the walls was peeling and the signs had definitely seen better days.

"Wait." Walter recognized the stop. "What are we doing here?"

Casey pulled up and took the keys out of ignition. "Come on."

Then without waiting for Walter to gather his bearings, Casey exited the truck.

There bell above the door jingled as the two brothers entered. There was a small line of patrons waiting to pay for their items. They pulled in a silently waited as some old country song played on the radio, echoing like tin through the rest stop, the fluorescent lights buzzing. Casey nudged Walter forward as the lined moved upstream.

An old man who appeared as though he was two steps away from death shakily turned some hot dogs on a grill. Nostalgia hit Walter, he recognized him. He could hardly believe this guy was still here. He had seemed ancient when they were kids, and now he was probably the oldest man in the county, yet there he was, still serving the same hot dogs. Casey watched him, he couldn't help drawing a parallel to his own situation at the plant.

Ahead of the brothers in line were two small dark-haired boys, punching each other's arms. Each taking turns and repeating "Punch, dead arm." The elder one giggled as he threw a merciless punch at his little brother. Their father ignored them as he stood at the counter paying the man. For a moment Walter stared at the two kids, like a mirror of their past. A reminder of the days before things had changed. He smiled fondly as they played. The little brother rubbing his arm.

"Hey, that hurt!"

The cry suddenly turned around their father, who scolded them both for misbehaving. Guilty, they held their heads low. Their father gave them each a little scruff on the head and handed them their hot dogs.

Casey and Walter exchanged glances. This was them once.

As he herded them out of the store, the father gave Casey and Walter a tired smile, pleased that they weren't bothered by his kid's behavior.

Casey and Walter stepped up to the counter.

A young cashier awaited them at the till with a pleasant smile.

"What will it be?"

"Three dogs each, with everything. You want anything else Walt?"

Walter shook his head, his skin heating up. He could feel himself flushing. He could hardly take his eyes off the girl behind the counter. She gave him a sweet smile, before turning and sliding the receipt to the old man, who squinted his eyes in strain, trying to read it.

The brothers stepped to the side and awaited their order. Walter leaned into Casey's ear.

"She's beautiful." He whispered.

Casey grinned. "Telling me doesn't do a whole lotta good. Tell her."

He nudged Walter in her direction, who seemed to be about in her twenties.

"She wouldn't go for someone like me." Walter paused, considering. "Why don't you tell her?"

"She's a bit young." Casey replied.

"Yeah, you're right, she's under fifty."

Casey had to hold back his smile. Admittedly, Walter had got him there. "You're not funny."

"She'd like you. Go on." Walter encouraged.

Just then she looked over at the two brothers staring at her. She had picked up a couple words from their conversation and shied away with a smile, her cheeks flushing slightly.

As the brother's grabbed their order and headed out, Casey exchanged a parting glance with the Cashier and even though they recognized a spark in one another, something that many of us have felt with a desirable stranger, they chalked it up as a fleeting moment of opportunity lost.

Minutes later, Casey pulled his truck into the marina's small parking lot, both had already started on their first hot dog.

"You should've said something." Walter remarked, his mouth full, with ketchup on the side of his lips.

"Fine. Okay. Thank you. I'll remember that next time." Casey replied dismissively before pointing to the back of the truck. "Grab your gear."

He took another bite of his hot dog and fishes his rod from the back.

"God damn that's good. Old man's got some gift."

Walter finished the remainder of his and wiped his hands on his pants.

"They were better before."

Still chewing Walter followed Casey, using his foot to stand on the truck's rear wheel and stretching inside to grab his gear.

"Are you kidding? They've always been the same."

"He used different buns." Walter replied unamused.

Casey stared in disbelief. "You remember the buns?"

Casey continued to walk ahead towards the marina docks, Walter's remark itched his memory, he realized that his brother was right, the old man did use different bread when they were kids, he turned and stared Walter, 'What else was trapped in his sense memory?'. Walter smiled as he struggled to match Casey's pace, he had brought the works, all his old fishing gear and was set to reel-in a Marlin. Eventually they reached their boat on one of the far arms of the marina. Walter slowed as the name of the vessel came within reading distance.

The Majestic

It sat amidst the other vessels, paint chipped and worn. Hearing them approach, Captain Kyle leaned out from the control room and waved them onboard, Kyle had been the skipper when their father worked this vessel, the years and a life on seas had not been kind to him.

Casey stepped on, loading his gear. Walter was stopped dead, his body feeling numb.

"Why are we taking this boat?"

Casey looked up from arranging his stuff. Took in Walter's expression for a second then replied.

"What's wrong with it?"

Walter continued to stare at Casey in disbelief. Was he really doing this?

"Take me home."

"Get on."

Walter was torn. He missed fishing, he wanted to go. The ocean lapped lightly against the side of the boat. Walter knew what Casey was trying to do. He felt suspended, trapped between two extremes.

Casey extended his hand.

"Come on, Walt."

Walter reluctantly handed Casey his rod and tackle gear and stepped onboard. He could hardly believe he took the step. But there he was. The familiar feeling underfoot and the slight sway from the ocean began to bring back old feelings.

Captain Kyle stepped out of the control room. "Hey guys. Excited?" They took in each other and how time had ravaged them all. "You boys, grew-up well." Kyle remarked, his words drowned in unease.

"Thank you, Captain." Walter nodded politely but quickly turned away, the Captain got a solid read on his expression. Kyle was intuitive and felt the tension in Walter's voice. He turned to Casey.

"The tank's full. Everything else, is like riding a bike." he assured.

Casey nodded in recognition of what the captain was doing, perhaps it was from the years of guilt, perhaps from an obligation to make things right. The nod also assured that Casey had this under control.

"Good luck fellas." He glanced at Walter, "Good luck, son." he stepped off the boat and left it Casey's hands.

Walter's trepidation began to surface as Casey slowly pulled The Majestic out from dock, leaving the land behind them. He stood at the bow nervously twitching his fingers whilst Casey did all the preliminary weather checks and navigation.

From the shore, the Majestic could be seen moving across the horizon. The weather was overcast but no risk of any sudden downpour or storm. Eventually she slowly drifted to a stop. Casey let down the anchor and The Majestic sat still upon the calm waters. Walter was struggling to keep his composure. Old feelings were swelling-up and clambering to the surface, things he wasn't sure he was ready to face. The desire to fish had completely disappeared, all Walter wanted to do was to return to shore. He looked around and sighed, down below was the blue-hole.

Casey arrived with his gear and noticed an irate Walter.

"Big surprise. We're fishing here."

Casey smiled and began to bait his lure.

"You remember this place?" Casey said while fishing for a worm.

Walter gave him a scowl.

"This is where you nearly drowned, isn't it?"

Fuming, Walter turned away from Casey. He'd had enough.

Casey cast his line. It soared long across the open sky. Pleased with himself he rested his rod against the boat and lay back.

Walter on the other hand was tensing even more. There was no way in hell he was fishing. Casey seeing this simply nodded a 'fine' and relaxed even further onto the boat chair.

Hours went by. The clouds glided gently across the sky, sifting seamlessly through one another. Casey wore his hat over his face and was half a step away from sleep, whilst his lure bobbed lightly in the calm ocean. Walter on the other hand was still stubbornly sat with his arms folded, glaring into the empty space before him. His emotions had been festering and mutating ever since he stepped foot aboard 'The Majestic'. In Walter's eyes this was all a complete waste of time, but he couldn't ignore the swelling fear that he was doing everything in his power not to confront the darkness that had destroyed him.

"Are you done?" Walter finally spoke. "I've gone through all of this exposure crap before. Dr. McKenzie brought me here, that hypnotist mom hired, and Dr. Wallace. It's useless, they got nothing from me then and you're not going to get anything from me now. You're wasting our time." Walter's face was weary, fighting the dread and ignoring the fear, which was consuming every ounce of energy he had. "Let's go home."

Casey sat up, removing the hat from his face and stared at his brother for a moment before speaking.

"You are home, Walt. Why else would I have forced you to say goodbye to mom? Maybe you were meant to die out here?"

Walter frowned, he appeared confused. "What?"

Casey stood up and walked towards the railing. Walter followed his brothers gaze to the dark blue hole sitting ominously, like a massive sea creature's jaws, waiting to swallow him up. Walter lost all the color in his face, frantically he glanced back and forth from Casey and the spot where he had nearly drowned all those years ago. He suddenly became aware of the fact that they were in the middle of the ocean and there was no easy way back to shore. Walter was trapped.

"Where do you think you can run, huh?" Casey said in a cool calm voice, leaning heavily against the railing of the boat.

Walter began to panic. He was searching everywhere for a way out, but there was nothing. Second by second Walter's choices thinned until he was left with only one option. Casey turned to look his brother in the eye. But, Walter was hardly present as memories began flooding back.

"Why are you doing this?" Walter posed the question as more of plea, a cry for help.

Casey didn't reply.

"I'm your brother, Casey!"

Casey took a long deep breath before speaking, and those few seconds stretched time. They wavered the lines of fear, amplifying Walter's tension.

"I'm *doing this*, Walt… Because, all you do is hurt us. You do it well. Mom had one wish, one thing she asked for."

"Fine. Take me back."

"Too late. Mom wants Walter back, not whoever you are. We lost Walter the day you drowned. You could've made that dive blindfolded! What happened down there?"

Walter didn't want to remember, he didn't want to dig through the muddy swell of his memory. But, Casey stared unrelenting and Walter could see that he had no other choice.

"Okay." Walter said, resignation in his voice. He stared into nothingness, his gaze shifted to the blue-hole beside them and just watched it, the moment felt like an eternity. "Half way in… something felt wrong, Casey. Like when your heart beats faster for no reason. I felt like I was losing air quicker than normal, and then I got this feeling… that something wasn't right. It happened just when I reached the opening of the cave." He paused. "I could see the surface getting further and further away… then, it went dark. And I woke up there on the deck." Walter stared at the area on the boat where life had returned to him.

Casey slowly nodded. Walter watched him, unsure, vulnerable and open.

"How far down did it happen? Show me."

Walter silently got up and walked past Casey and towards the bow. Quietly he pointed towards a section of water. He was about to turn around when his world started falling. No. He was falling.

Casey shoved Walter into the ocean.

In the control room an alarm triggered. Sirens blared, a warning reading 'man overboard' flashed incessantly. Casey rushed to a panel and slammed a 'cut-off' button. The siren stopped.

Walter struggled to get his bearings and grasp what had just happened. He wadded water, gulping down air as Casey watched from above, blank and cold hearted.

"What the hell is wrong with you?!"

"D'you remember what the Captain said? 'Bring back a souvenir.' And look what you brought back! Nothing but grief."

Walter was speechless. His eyes shifting from Casey's to the blue-hole below him. Walter couldn't believe this was actually happening His own brother had thrown him into his biggest trauma, it was a miracle that he was still afloat. Anger began to swell up, and the anger over-whelmed the fear.

"Here." Casey said, tossing a float. "Help yourself out."

It landed right in front of him, splashing Walter in the face.

As it landed, something switched in Walter's head. He scowled at it, humiliated and bitter. Sick of everything that he'd had to endure. Sick of his brother, sick of this damn hole in the ocean. What he did next sur-prised both Casey and himself. He took a deep breath, then dove down, leaving the float drifting aimlessly out and away from The Majestic.

Casey knew he had crossed the line. Not only had he crossed it but he had sailed leagues past it. All in one moment. It had happened so fast, like something and seized control of him. Now as the only sounds were that of the gulls circling and the sea crashing against the boat, the fire in his mind began to extinguish. Shaking off the feeling, he watched and waited for Walter to surface.

He waited and waited.

"Christ!!" He said out loud, anxiety taking over. "Walter!" Casey screamed into the ocean. He could no longer see his brother's body.

~

Walter swam, heading deeper and deeper towards the reef floor. There was a determination in his bones that he hadn't felt in years, decades. The world down here was peaceful, an ambrosial weightlessness of silent landscapes. Walter struggled through the pain as the dark abyss dawned nearer and nearer. His heartbeat began to rise again, just as it had done before.

Casey was pacing anxiously on the top deck, frequently checking his watch. Walter had been gone for far too long. He began to panic. This was his doing, his fault, if anything happened to Walter, Casey would not be able to live with himself. He would be his brother's killer. Worry and guilt ate at him until Casey could face them no longer. He braced himself and dove in head first after Walter.

Walter neared the base of the reef. He could feel the power draining from his muscles as he used up all his oxygen, he could feel himself growing weaker and his vision began to blur around the edges. Under all the strain, boundaries of the mind and the physical world were broken. Memories began to appear in the ocean around him. They played in silent reply.

He saw his mother sleeping across two visitor chairs. He saw himself in the hospital after his accident. Clearly, she had been there all night, waiting for him to awake.

The memories came and went like evaporations, bleeding into one another. Like smoke in the water, another memory would surface.

Walter shops with June. There is another man there, the meeting appears co-incidental. His name is Derek. Derek buys his mom jewelry. Derek buys him a football.

Then motel room walls rose-up and Walter is babysitting Casey. June pokes her head around the corner and makes sure they are okay. Derek unbuttons his shirt.

The doctors tell Walter to remain still as they scan his brain. Walter doesn't understand why his mom couldn't be in there with him. They watch him through the glass window. His mom holds Casey close. Walter wishes she was holding him. His father remains distant, his eyes a haunting sight of guilt.

More doctors. So many doctors. Check-ups, post check-ups, tests, scans. A bright light shines into Walter's eyes. Derek moves it away. Derek is his doctor and educated everyone on Walter's condition.

Hypoxia.

The word hits him like an eighteen-wheeler truck.

His dad leaves, he cannot bare seeing Walter like this.

Walter's parents fight. There is always a fight now, for the smallest reason. Walter fears that it's because of him they are fighting. Perhaps he mentioned Derek's gifts, he cannot remember. Now, Walter whispers important things three times, three times, three times… making sure they're stuck.

His dad is no longer his dad. His dad was his rock. He's now always onboard 'The Majestic', always working, absent from their lives.

Hospital rooms. Therapists. Bright flicking fluorescent lights. Needles and pills that make him feel like a fragment of himself. Always dazed. Drooling. Removed.

Walter's dad is now gone. They said he accidently went overboard during a catch and rough seas swallowed him whole.

But Walter knows the truth, his dad killed himself.

It was Walter's fault.

His mom cries at the funeral. Casey cries. Walter wants to but cannot, he's dazed and only feels guilt.

This is his fault.

A scream ripped through Walter's throat as he yelled the memories away. He pushed himself further, swimming deeper.

Casey swam towards him, struggling more than he anticipated. His lungs were already burning, his body convulsing, fighting to drink in air. But the surface was too far now, it was too late to turn back.

With a final kick Walter made it to the entrance of the blue hole. Clawing at the sand, his fingers grabbed hold of a rock on the reef floor. A calm washed over him. The throbbing in his ears and the pain in his lungs stopped hurting. It became only a sensation, a distant feeling. He turned and planted his feet on the sand. Looking up to the wavering surface he saw Casey's body as a stark shadow, blurry and undefined. The surface seemed as if it were miles away. Walter's body was weak. He was about to kick off, when a voice from behind turned him around. 'Walter' came the voice again. His father's voice. It was coming from deep within the blue hole. Walter whipped towards its source, and shimmering like a mirage Douglas was smiling and waving for Walter to come deeper, to come join him.

Walter floated, suspended as if in space, watching his father's image. He looked-up to see if Casey could see him as well, but then Walter's heart sunk. Casey was grasping his throat, choking, trying to tear his way back up to the surface. Walter instantly kicked off from the reef floor. Just as he did, another memory flashed before him.

It was the day everything changed, the last time they were here. He saw Casey struggling above him, running out of air. Young Walter rushed towards his little brother. As he swam towards him, Walter did so in the present as well. The silhouette of Casey shifted back and forth, from young to old. Both, fighting for their life.

Two men burst through the ocean's surface.

Two boys burst through the ocean's surface.

Time replayed itself. The past and present wove themselves like a tapestry, until one could not be distinguished from the other. A fisherman swam towards them. Walter had rescued Casey.

That was the truth.

The truth that Walter had displaced, lost in shroud of guilt and mind-numbing drugs.

Young Walter lost consciousness as he surfaced, but his younger brother gasped for air.

This time around the past left itself behind. Walter inhaled life back into his lungs and dragged his unconscious brother through the ocean.

With one free hand, Walter clambered up the ladder of 'The Majestic', hoisting his brother up with him. As they landed on the deck, without hesitation Walter went to work resuscitating Casey, pressing his palms repeatedly on his chest and feeding him air.

Moments later Casey coughed, spitting out a profuse amount of water. His eyes narrowed their focus and saw the weary face of Walter, who slumped back, leaning against the deck, exhausted and drained.

"What the hell were you thinking? You nearly killed us." The words came slow and calm from Walter.

Casey looked away.

"Why?"

Casey spared a side glance at his brother and reading the expression on his face he knew that Walter remembered the truth of what had happened.

"You didn't save me, Casey."

He looked for a way to reply, guilt and apology was written over his face. But the emotions overwhelmed him, they choked his words and only tears managed to escape.

"You kept up the lie… all these years?"

Casey broke down, tears streamed down his face.

"I was a hero. Mom and dad both thanked me. Dad thanked me? When did they ever look at me that way?"

Walter watched his brother with glassy eyes. He should've been bitter, angry, after all he was betrayed by one person who meant to be in his corner, who simply stood by and watched him drown for years in psychiatric institutions and therapy sessions. But, what would that accomplish? Walter let go of any hate, regret and any other illusion of the ego that would jeopardize mending their wounds. His demeanor reflected that he understood.

"I've lived my whole life with that lie. It destroyed us, destroyed mom and dad. No matter how much I wanted to tell you, her… a lie never washes clean."

Walter's gaze dropped from his brother's hysteria.

"And it doesn't die, it returns with a wrath. A lie takes vengeance through people you love."Casey trailed off. Walter reflected on his words, perhaps he meant his relationship with Julia and its foundation of lies, perhaps he meant his so-called best friends or their mom's infidelity with Derek.

Walter could see the hell Casey lived in and it mirrored his own.

Both brothers slowly looked up and took each other in. They had witnessed themselves hit rock bottom, the lowest of the lows, and in this moment, all they had was one another.

Walter offered an empathic smile.

"For the record. Its two-nil, hero."

A small smile, like the early morning light, slowly spread across Casey's cheeks. Walter mirrored his brother. The light continued to grow and eventually a laugh broke over the horizon. Both brothers laughed in the face of death as they sat drenched and exhausted on 'The Majestic'. Once again, at the mouth of the blue hole. The tides of time had come full circle.

Casey picked himself up and took a moment to rest his palm on Walter's shoulder. For a moment they reflected on what had just happened, reflected on their life and what all this meant moving forward.

Casey moved towards the control room and peacefully tuned the boat around. In no rush he steered 'The Majestic' at a snail's pace, taking in the surrounding ocean and landscape, the rays of light filtering through the clouds and glinting off the shimmering sea. The gulls dancing above held a new meaning, their patterns of flight crisscrossing and interviewing like stanzas in a poem. To both brothers, it seemed as if God was stretching down from his place in heaven and lighting the way forward.

Silence was the unspoken thread that held the brothers together. They shared glances with one another, conveying more than words ever could. Something had changed. They both could feel it as the wind blew in their hair and the shore grew bigger and bigger before them, as if it were arriving to welcome them, and not the other way around.

The silence stretched as they tied 'The Majestic' to the dock and walked the old planks of wood back to Casey's truck. On the drive back home, the brother could feel that whilst they had taken a huge step in healing the schism that kept them separate and distant, there was still a lot to be dealt with and naturally it would take time for the rift to be sealed.

They entered their family home. Shoes still wet, were discarded by the front door. Walter was the first to break the silence.

"Casey." Walter said, his brother turning in response. "I'm gonna go back. Sort things out in Seattle."

Casey nodded. "Good."

"I'd like to come back. Maybe live here, when the time's right."

"This is your home, Walt."

Walter nodded slowly, letting those words sink in. Casey turned and headed to his room.

"Casey?"

He glanced back over his shoulder at Walter who stared directly in his eyes. Then slowly Walter walked towards him and before Casey could fully process what was happening Walter's arms were around him, pulling Casey close and hugging him tight.

It took Casey by surprise. The warmth, the love. Memories of them as children playing together rushed back. Where had they all vanished? Casey in his tunnel reverie didn't even have time to lift his arms in return but Walter understood.

They hadn't hugged in a decade.

Casey smiled a weary, labored smile, exhaustion and guilt still weighing on his heart.

CHAPTER NINE

The sun had risen over an hour ago and the majority of residents within Westport were awake and preparing for the day ahead.

Casey peaked into Walter's room and was taken aback at the image before him. Walter stood by his dresser, combing through his hair. This was the cleanest and most well-dressed Casey had seen his brother in a long time. Even his hair had a fresh cut and was newly dyed.

"Hey Walt, I'm off to work."

"Okay. I hope you don't mind, I went and picked-up a few things."

Casey lightly shook his head, a proud smile lifting on his cheeks.

"Not at all. You look good."

"Thanks." Walter replied, feeling calm with who he was today. That life would be manageable.

"You're not on your way to ask out that cashier, are you?"

Walter smiled, glancing across to Casey.

"Maybe. So, you better hurry-up."

Casey chuckled a little and waved a hand. "See you later, Walt."

The sound of the door closing marked Casey's departure. Walter set down the comb on the dresser beside him and absorbed his new reflection in the mirror. He felt confident, happy with the way he looked. It felt like a lifetime, since he'd seen this version of himself.

Meanwhile at the tuna plant, Casey strode out of the elevator with an air of confidence and composed authority. Gene noticed him the minute he stepped out.

"Casey, good to have you back."

"Thanks, Gene."

Gene studied him, looking for any tells that signaled instability.

"So, you are back?"

"I'm back."

Gene relaxed, "How's your family doing?"

"Good actually. Things are looking better."

Gene smilingly offered him his clipboard. Unlike before Casey wasn't hesitant as he nodded. "Sure." And took over the clipboard. Gene could feel the shift in Casey, and walked away, confident with him managing the floor.

Without hesitation Casey began calling out the list of people on the clipboard, double checking the factory line to make sure they were present. He watched Julia the same amount of time as he did the rest. She felt coldness in his stare and her smiled dropped, she motioned with her head to a private area. She wanted to talk. But Casey lightly shook his head, now wasn't the time. Hector waved to him from beside Julia and left his position, walking over to Casey.

"Hey Case, good to have you back. How's your brother doing?"

"He's fine."

"Must be hard taking care of him by yourself."

"It's not actually."

"I mean… It must be hard on your love life. You guys don't get much privacy, huh?"

Casey didn't respond. But Julia abruptly strode off, heading towards the restrooms, Casey's eyes wandered from Hector. He watched her with concern as she disappeared behind the door. No. He couldn't let her take his attention away from work. He returned his gaze to his clipboard, ignoring Hector's last statement. Hector however didn't move, he leaned in closer so that no one could hear what he was about to say.

"You need to give us overtime, man. Now."

The comment caught Casey off-guard, he stared at Hector.

"She's a great woman." He continued.

It took Casey a moment to realize who he was referring to.

"A bit older than my taste but I can see the kick. You're her supervisor, her husband will shoot you if ever he found out, risky man."

Casey was speechless as Hector's intentions sank in. "Are you gonna be a good boy, Casey?"

Casey stared at Hector coldly. What did he expect him to do, invent a new salary just for him?

"You're not this dumb Hector." Casey paused. "Well maybe you are but, it's not happening."

Hector looked frustrated, envy seethed in his voice. "We're your best friends, Casey. We both know that I should've gotten that promotion. I was the one who got you this job, I brought you in here."

Casey rose his eyebrows staring hard at his so-called friend.

"Look. Just do what you're told. Keep banging her. Don't rock the boat."

"I… Let me see, what I can do."

Hector smiled a disconcerting smile, he playfully slapped Casey and left for the production line.

Casey knew that trusting Hector was like confiding a secret in a news bulletin, Hector would leverage as much as he could to steal as much as he could, from him, the plant, even Julia. Right now, he wanted overtime but what would he demand next? Hector worked away on the production line with his sycophant, Dave. The wicked sneer of victory plastered on their faces.

Casey stormed off towards his office, and unbeknownst to him Julia was behind him, running to catch-up.

"Casey."

Her voice stopped him right in his tracks. He took a deep breath and sighed. She was the last person he wanted to see right now.

"Julia, please, I don't have time now."

He was half way through turning back to his office when she grabbed his arm.

"We need to talk. It's important."

She removed her hand and Casey noticed her fingers trembling with nervousness. Her whole posture was guarded and revealed that it would not be an easy conversation.

"What is it?"

Julia spared glances around her to make sure no one was within an ear's distance.

"I think John knows about us."

It was precisely the good news he was expecting. A sinking feeling of dread fell upon Casey as the words came out of her mouth. He always knew this day would come, but had pushed that thought to the back of his mind every time it arose. Guilt and anxiety were written plainly in her eyes and it mirrored Casey. He did his best to keep a blank face and to not scream at the top of his lungs.

"Are you sure?"

"He saw a strange number on the phone bill. Apparently, we used to call each other a lot, Casey."

"Christ. Did you come-up with something?"

"I told him it was Patrick's friend, but..."

Casey interrupted. "I know John isn't the smartest cop in the world, but couldn't you come up with a better lie?"

"He took me by surprise, I had to think on the spot. That was the first thing... Look, it doesn't matter. Maybe you shouldn't be seen with me anymore."

"You think?!"

Julia lets the aggression fly past. She knew what Casey was going through, she knew all the troubles he had on his plate. She offered him a sympathetic look. There was still affection there for him. Casey could see that this hurt her as much as it hurt him. He immediately regretted losing his cool. She didn't deserve that.

Meanwhile at their home, Walter was attempting to cook steak when the phone rang. He wiped his hands on his mom's apron and picked-up the receiver.

"Hello? — Hi. Dr. McKenzie. Yes, thanks for returning my call. — Yeah, things are good. Really good. — I'd like to talk to you as well. — Yes."

Feeling something like a resolution Walter returned to his cooking, finishing the sear on his steak. He switched off the heat on the roasted vegetables and plated himself. As he sat down to eat, the phone rang again. Probably Dr. McKenzie, he thought.

"Hello?" There was no answer. "Hello?" Walter tried again. 'Dr. Mckenzie?"

The monotonous beep of the line going dead was the only answer that came. Walter looked at the old cell phone confused before hanging-up and returning to his meal.

At the police station, John Griffin placed the phone down on the table and stared blankly at the wall ahead of him. Something in his heart snapped, as the reality of the situation settled in. He frowned and fought through the tears, not letting a single one escape, bottling his emotions. He set his jaw, clenching his teeth together. He was a man after all.

"Shake it off, John." He whispered to himself.

"Shake it off."

The late afternoon sun gleamed. Heavy rays of sun stretching down and reflecting off the dark sunglasses of two electrical workers. They walked towards the side of the Treggar family home. The senior supervisor took a reading of the electrical box as his apprentice leaned against the wall smoking a cigarette, obviously bored by the day's work and reluctant to show much effort, he stared at the ocean swell with longing, dreaming about turning pro. The readings were normal and the supervisor motioned with his head to move on to the next house. The trainee electrician sighed and flicked his cigarette. They walked off, attending to all the other houses in the vicinity.

The cigarette continued to turn on the ground, smoldering by small pieces of bark. A discarded aerosol can lay inches away.

Walter was fast asleep in his room when the smoke began to engulf the house.

Back at the plant the finishing bell rung obnoxiously and workers sighed in relief that the day had ended. Casey turned to watch the bell ringing. The more he watched the less sound he heard. Until the bell became a muted numbness in his ears, the frantic back and forth of the trigger hitting its shell.

Casey pulled up to his house, greeted by the blinding blue and red lights of an ambulance. A massive fire truck took up the majority of the road so Casey had to park behind it. Walter was unconscious on a stretcher as the paramedics carried him from the scorched house, an oxygen mask over his face.

Casey fought his way through the crowd of onlookers and the murmuring of voices. He tried to run to Walter but a fireman stopped him before he could get close.

"Wait! This is my house!" His eyes wouldn't pry from Walter. "Is he alright?!"

The fireman did his best to calm Casey down. "He's gonna be fine."

The doors to the ambulance closed and the siren turned on as it sped away into the distance, the lights scarred themselves into his retina as he watched it go.

"How… How did this happen."

"Ask the chief." The fireman pointed over towards one of the firemen who stood on the porch, talking with his crew and police officers.

Casey ran up to them. "What happened?"

The chief held up an aerosol can.

No.

This wasn't happening.

"Someone threw a match or cigarette out the window." The chief continued. "It caught light on dry wood chips. The rest you can piece together."

Casey nodded. "Thanks."

He stumbled back, taking in the aftermath of the charred house. The damage was heavy but not irreparable. Casey stood dumbfounded, a mix of rage and grief all together. He genuinely thought Walter was better, that his recovery could be been a silver lining of hope for their mother, but since their return life had other plans, dealing out one blow after another.

Eventually the firemen cleared and the crowd of onlookers disappeared with them. Casey sat on the stairs of his front porch, staring down at the ground when his phone rang.

Through a small observation window, Casey watched quietly as Walter lay expressionless, face towards the ceiling, limbs strapped to the bed. Heather appeared next to him and lay a hand on his back to show her solidarity. Casey managed to peel his eyes away for a moment and returned a smile and some recognition. He really did appreciate it.

"It's for the best, Casey. He could have been seriously injured."

"I know… I just thought that he was actually getting better."

"Most people in recovery show temporary signs of rehabilitation, but… more often or not they relapse."

"Can I speak to him?"

She looked at him like she wasn't supposed to say yes, but nodded. "Be quick."

Casey's hand reached for the door handle and hesitated, hovering over it for a moment. He couldn't believe he was in this situation again. The disappointment was heavy as he finally opened the door and stepped inside.

Walter didn't move or show any sign of acknowledgement that Casey was present. He watched him for a while, then Walter spoke.

"I didn't do it."

"I know."

Walter's eyes moved for the first time to read Casey's expression.

"You were really lucky, Walt."

"I didn't start that fire, Casey!"

"It's fine, Walt."

"Stop. Doing *that*. Playing the shrink."

Casey shook his head in disappointment. It was just like before.

"Y'know you really fooled me. I thought you'd gotten well."

"I am Case. you have to get me out of here. I don't know how that fire got started, but it wasn't me."

"This is for the best, Walt."

"Wait, no. Casey. No. Untie these."

"These people will keep you safe"

"Casey! No! Get me out of here! I'm not crazy!"

Walter struggled and fought against his restraints, shaking the bed and groaning in frustration. Leather ties would make anyone react like Walter did. Freedom is the biggest thing you can take from someone, and Walter knew he was innocent.

Casey watched his brother fight. It made everything grow cold and numb.

Walter managed to take a couple breaths and calmed himself. Seeing that his outrage was not helping his case.

In an even tone Walter tried to appeal to Casey again. "I want to see mom. I need to tell her something."

Casey shook his head. In his eyes, Walter was using any excuse he could to free himself. Casey didn't feel the sincerity in his brother's voice, nor did he see the truth in his eyes, he was numb and nothing Walter said would change anything.

"I'm sorry Walt. It's too late for that now."

Casey gave his brother one last look before leaving.

Before he reached the door, he heard his brother crying.

"Please Casey. Help me."

The words hung in the air, heavy with tears and sorrow but Casey's heart had turned black. He didn't even glance back as he shut the door and left.

"Casey! No! Casey!"

Walter incessantly yelled after his brother, his haunting pleas followed Casey all the way down the hall, out the building and clawed themselves in his mind..

CHAPTER TEN

◆◇◆

In the low light of Motel 8's cheapest room, Casey sipped absently on an even cheaper whisky. Valerie Stevens was by the bed putting her clothes back on. She was a kind woman in her sixties, age had done her well. She had stayed away from tabacco and alcohol and it was evident in her skin. Casey had remembered her visiting his mother when Walter had arrived and it was easy falling back in her arms.

"Come home with me sweetie. You're upset. June will be fine, long as I've known her she's been a fighter."

In Casey's mind it took a while for the words to settle and a couple more moments to process what he should do, the whisky slowing his cognition. Eventually he nodded and offered her an appreciative drunken smile. But his eyes didn't meet hers, they returned to the same spot on the floor a moment later. Valerie watched him with pity. She knew what it was like to lose a parent. Heck, she was sixty years old, she had been through her share of heartbreak.

"Come on. Grab your things. You're coming with me."

"I'm fine."

Pursing her lips and raising her eyebrows as if to say 'yeah right', Valerie stood there with her arms folded waiting to see if Casey would say anything more. She knew when someone didn't want to be helped and she wasn't going to mother him, he was a grown man and could make his own bad choices.

"Alright Casey. If you need anything, feel free to stop by."

Casey could only muster half a nod. She sighed and left, leaving Casey alone to wallow in self-pity. The door closed silently behind her. Once she had left emotions burst to the surface, emotions Casey had been hiding, emotions he could not let others see. Emotions so strong that Casey feared if he released them, he would tear the room apart. So, he kept them distance, locked up and screamed in silence.

~

Walter stared into nothing. The nurses voices were distant and muted.

"Is he…"

"Yeah, he's alive. Was he like this when you found him?"

"Yes. He was just staring at the ceiling. He hasn't blinked or responded to a word I've said."

Maybe this is what it felt like to be a ghost, Walter thought.

A female voice spoke.

"Give him a shower. It'll also help if you walked him around."

Two staff members nodded, complying to the instructions.

"Come on Walter. Let's get you clean." The man's face that appeared above Walter was smiling. It was the same staff member who's nose Walter had broken. "You remember me, handsome? It's Phil."

Walter blinked, his eyes scanning the man's face.

"Oh yeah, he remembers you." A nearby colleague chimed.

Phil helped Walter up while Donnie held the wheelchair steady.

Walter barely had the will to hold his own head up as Phil wheeled him down an endless corridor. Every turn this way or that lolled Walters head from side to side. Phil and Donnie talked with one another but none of their words made any sense.

Come on Walter. Pull it together. You have to pull it together.

Walter managed to find an ounce of strength and sat up a little straighter. If he had any chance of getting out of here, he was going to have to act normal.

As they wheeled him into the shower room, Walter signaled with his hand for them to stop. Phil raised an eyebrow and watched as Walter got up and undressed himself. He knew the drill. He was going to be monitored the whole time. This wasn't anything new.

He let the water run hot on his skin, the steam quickly filling the room. The constant cascade of the shower on his face soothed him, and the heat brought some feeling into his cold body. Then, for a bit of fun he turned around and looked at Phil in the eye as he soaped himself. Phil smiled and unconsciously bit his lip.

"So, you're not as gone as we thought."

Walter closed his eyes and looked up towards the steam of water again. He needed time to think, to clear the fog the medication left him in. This was the perfect opportunity. Before they fed him more drugs, before he was surrounded by all the real patients. He needed to speak to Casey, had to try and explain himself.

"Alright, times up shower boy."

Phil insisted that he be wheeled back to his room and Walter didn't protest. He needed to do everything possible to show these people that he was fine. At the end of the hallway, Heather Mazzanno was giving a tour to a prospective patient. As they neared her Walter reached out to get her attention.

"Ms Mazzanno?"

Heather stopped mid-sentence.

"Yes Walter?" But before Walter could say what he wanted, Heather turned to the man she was guiding. "Walter is one of our more 'unique' patients."

Walter forced a smile in the man's direction before addressing heather again.

"I would like to make a phone call."

"Okay. And who would you like to call?"

"My brother. I'd like to find out about our mom. You know she's been sick lately."

Heather smiled politely, and replied in an overly understanding voice that so many doctors used with him. "Oh yes, of course." She motioned to the staff, giving them the green light. "I hope everything is fine with her and you reach your brother without any trouble. But, I must be off now."

Mirroring her sentiment, Walter politely thanked her.

~

Casey stood in front of the Southern Marine Tuna Plant workers for the first time as their official boss. They murmured amongst one another at the state of him. Casey knew he looked like hell, but he ignored their small comments and continued roll-call, focusing only on the list before of him.

"Dion Henshaw."

"Here."

Casey ticked him off.

"Rodney Palmer."

"Yeah."

Tick.

"Hector Lewis."

There was silence. Casey had to look up from his clipboard. Hector was there. He nodded. Casey had to restrain himself from snapping his pencil in two.

Tick.

The pencil lead crumbled slightly as Casey pushed down heavily on the paper, barely holding in his frustration.

"Dave Larkin."

Casey ticked the notepad before anyone spoke, but the reply still came.

"Here, boss."

"Julia Griffin."

"Here."

Casey didn't make eye contact with her, he didn't even bother to look up from the list. Julia's heart sank as she noticed. What did she expect, this was how it had to be from here on out.

"Alright. Everyone file in. By the way, the overtime schedule's up. Don't be late."

The group disbursed, muttering to themselves as they headed towards the production line. Hector and Dave celebrated, their names clearly written at the top of the overtime schedule. They didn't even acknowledge Casey, basking in their victory. He watched them, betrayal leaving a bitter taste in his mouth.

He could feel Julia's sympathetic gaze on him. He ignored her.

On the way back to his office, a worker approached Casey with a phone, his hand over the receiving end, to mute the factory noise. Casey mouthed a 'thank you' and took it from him.

"Hello, Casey Treggar."

"Casey?"

He sighed. "What is it Walter?"

"I want to see mom."

"Fine. I'll come by later."

Looking up Casey spotted Gene, he appeared to be leading a group of foreigners that looked important, giving them a rundown of the factory.

"I want to see her now Casey. I have a bad feeling."

"I'm busy…"

"There's something I need to tell her!"

"— Fine. I've got to go."

The line went silent for a moment. A raw silence that was tender with pain and betrayal.

"Casey…"

Walter needed to tell Casey something as well. He rested his head on the wall as he tried to gather up the courage. Phil snapped his fingers.

"Chop chop. Wrap it up."

Walter anxiously glanced at Phil and Donnie.

Casey became frustrated, waiting for Walter to speak. He discreetly glanced at Gene and saw him staring directly at Casey from across the plant.

"I'll come by later Walt. — Bye."

As Casey went to hang-up, he heard Walter on the other line.

"Casey?"

The sound of his name in Walter's mouth broke his heart. For a second Casey fought the urge to answer him, to leave the plant right then and remove Walter from of that damn institution. But, reluctantly the colder part won the battle and Casey hung-up.

The phone went dead in Walter's ear. The beeping became a drone, and Walter stood frozen for a long time after Casey had gone, letting the beeping numb his mind. Defeat sunk into his bones. Everything became heavy and sluggish. Eventually, Phil coaxed him away and took the phone from Walter's hands, checking with his own ear to make sure the line was cut before returning it to the receiver.

"Alright Walter. Let's get you to your room." Phil said.

Walter knew the drill, besides, he was in no mood to resist. Both staff members led him to his room and secured him onto the bed. They stood over him, talking amongst themselves, but making sure Walter could hear every word.

"He looks different, doesn't he? Like he's running for mayor." Sneered Donnie.

Walter stared into oblivion, ignoring the staff.

Donnie smiled at Phil, then motioned with his head in Walter's direction.

Phil returned the smile and pulled out a baton.

"Did you think I'd just forget, handsome?"

Donnie moved over and placed a phonebook on Walter's crotch. Without warning Phil brought the baton down as hard as he could. Whack!

The pain shocked through Walter's system like an electrical surge, causing his eyes to budge, his pupils dilating. Walter clenched his teeth, taking the blow. He was not going to give in, show them any pain.

Whack! Whack! Whack! The baton came down hard, beating him successively. One after another Walter took the blows. He could hardly breathe, his body tensing in fear and trauma. Walter did all he could to show no pain, but his eyes revealed everything, and his wardens reveled in it, fed off it.

Walter's body began to go into survival mode. His arms and legs pulling against the straps, trying to squeeze free, trying to escape. He shook the pain and replaced it with anger. Growling at them. The wardens both laughed, sharing the pleasure with one another. In their distraction they didn't notice Walter's arm had managed to weasel its way out. In one swift movement he grabbed a metal tray on the table beside him and swung. Whack!

It crashed into Donnie's head. Dazed and stunned, he stumbled backwards. Phil sprung to attention and was half in shock as his eyes darted back and forth between Walter and his colleague. Before Phil could react, Walter threw a powerful punch that hit him square in the nose, breaking it again with a horrible crack. Feral and surging with adrenaline Walter undid the remaining straps just as Donnie drunkenly regained his senses. Walter sprung out of bed and threw a knockout blow that squared his assailant directly in the temple. Donnie slapped against the floor unconscious. Phil held his nose, panic and anger in his eyes as blood gushed down his face. He scurried to the corner of the room, like a trapped animal.

"You psycho. You broke my nose… again! You'll pay!"

But, the orderly was in no position to be hurling threats. Walter smiled a twisted smile and fear truly settled in Phil's eyes.

When Walter had finished, he looked rather pleased with his handy work. Both the orderlies were strapped to the bed, one on top of the other, bare ass naked. Walter shoved a gag into their mouths and covered them with white bedding. Picking out the uniforms that weren't covered in blood, Walter dressed himself in them. He hung a jacket over the bedhead, blocking the view to the sleeping patient on the bed, trying not to attract the attention of a nurse.

He used a towel to hide his face, eluding that he had been injured by a patient. He went straight in the direction of the exit. *Dammit.* He muttered as his group therapist stepped into the corridor. She looked at him confused and unsure, but Walter pressed on. His only mistake was glancing back. She caught his eyes and immediately knew something was wrong. She quickly made her way to Walter's room. She was only a few feet away. Walter had to think fast. There. He pulled the fire alarm, and in an instant the whole building was wailing an alert.

Walter's therapist stopped a hair's breadth away from the door, responding to the alarm. Then the entire hall filled with patients poking their heads out of their rooms and stepping out into the hallway confused.

Walter strode away from the building, he was far enough now that no one would notice him, the alarm blared. He could already hear the sirens of a firetruck responding.

~

"Casey! Gene wants you."

Casey raised his eyebrows. He could tell by the man's expression that something was wrong. Gene sat at his desk behind a wall of paperwork. Two men sat across from him. The scene was grim as Casey knocked lightly at the open door.

"Come in Casey."

The men in the chairs were the electrical workers from the other day. They both looked guilty.

"This is Mr. Marshall and his assistant." Gene explained.

"They've got something to tell you."

~

Walter had made good progress. The psychiatric institution was long gone but Walter hadn't lessened his quick pace as he made his way down the country road towards the main hospital. He had his head down and hands planted in his pocket. The sound of a car neared and Walter did his best not to appear suspicious, but that was hard to do on a main road with no sidewalks and wearing all white.

Officer Griffin sped towards the psychiatric institute, with a new recruit in the passenger's seat. His fresh uniform still crisp and name tag shiny, which read Thomas Derby, he appeared as though a sixteen-year-old playing cop at Halloween.

The police department had just received a disturbing call from the institution's head of affairs, Ms. Heather Mazzanno. As they drove, John noticed a man walking alone on the opposite side of the road. Instantly he recognized his posture and demeanor. Walter kept his head to the ground as the car flew past.

He let out a sigh of relief and picked up his pace. Officer Griffin however, slowed down and swiftly turned the car around, trailing after Walter at a snail's pace. Just then his police radio sparked to life. The dispatch officer Deborah was on the other side.

"Suspect is a Walter Treggar, and is wearing a staff uniform."

Officer Griffin picked up the police radio and replied. "We're on him now."

The cop car crawled along silently following Walter, a shark stalking its prey. Once he got close enough, John switched his siren on. Like a deer in headlights Walter snapped his head towards them.

"Walter!" Officer Griffin ordered through a megaphone. "Stop. Get on the ground. This is your last…"

Walter turned and ran, sprinting with all his life away from the cop car.

Officer Griffin tossed the megaphone to his partner and slammed on the acceleration.

His partner, fresh out of bootcamp, reveled in the action, reality was better than any computer game. Officer Griffin screeched their vehicle to a halt, a few feet in front of Walter cutting off his escape. Both of the officers jumped out, guns drawn.

"Stop!"

Seeing the weapons, Walter immediately froze in his tracks.

"Hands where I can see them, Walter!"

Out of options Walter caught John's eyes.

"Please. I just want to see my mom."

"Hands! Now!"

Reluctantly Walter raised his hands into the air.

"Please, just take me to her."

"Get on the ground!"

Walter stayed standing. "Please, I need to see her."

"On the ground! Now!"

The Young cop shook from the adrenaline, the gun quivering in his hands.

Walter sighed. Lowering his hands.

"Walter! Get on the…"

He stepped forward.

Bang!

The newbie, Tom, fired his gun.

The air was sucked right out of Walter's lungs as the bullet hit him straight in the chest. Almost instantly, blood began to seep through his white shirt. Officer Griffin's mouth dropped open. He was speechless as he turned to his partner. Tom, looked as shocked as his superior officer. He stared at his gun in disbelief, his hands shaking like an earthquake, ringing in his ears.

Walter fell to the ground, his vision blurring in and out of focus as the bright blue sky soared endlessly above him. Puffy clouds gently drifted across, and flights of birds migrated in formation as the golden hour quickly approached.

As his senses returned, Officer Griffin shook his partner back to the present.

"Call an ambulance!"

Tom unfroze and rushed off into the police cruiser, still in a daze, still unable to believe what had happened. A pool of blood grew around Walter and trickled towards the wheel of Officer Griffin's police car.

"Mom…" Walter whispered, drifting in and out of consciousness. He stared towards the sky. "Mom."

June's eyes flickered open in her hospital bed. Her brows furrowed, tightly together in grief. "Walter?" Her voice barely audible was dry and raspy from disuse.

The sky disappeared and a memory flashed before Walter's eyes.

Walter climbed on his mom's shoulders, Casey still a little infant in her arms. They laughed and played, baby Casey reaching towards his brother with a toothless grin.

June smiled as she remembered the same thing. Her eyes yet mixed with sadness and joy.

"I'm sorry baby."

Walter tried to smile, whilst his body convulsed from the loss of blood. His lips creeped up slightly. A crow cawed somewhere in the distance. Tom was yelling their location to the emergency dispatch. Then, in one last exhale, the last slip of life escaped Walter's body. He went limp and his eyes became hollow.

Walter had died with his mother's voice in his ear. That was all he wanted. To hear her one last time. To feel the love, she had for him. The smile was frozen on his face as Officer Griffin hurried over in distress.

Somewhere in the distance a bell rang.

Then the world rushed into silence.

~

Everything was muted as Casey ran through the entrance to the hospital.

At the end of the hall he could see Officer Griffin and his partner staring blankly at the wall. As he ran towards them the fluorescent lights sparked and stuttered above. A nurse rose to meet him. She knew who he was. He couldn't hear the words that come out of her mouth, but read the expression on her face.

The world paused before the yelling began. Casey lost himself in the tidal wave of emotions. Tears broke from his eyes, gushing endlessly. His own screams drowned by the silence of grief as they left his mouth. A security guard approached him empathetically. Casey fought his way past him, charging towards the officers. They jumped up and restrained him, as Casey swung his fists blindly at them. The world around him spun, ceasing to make sense.

He didn't know when it happened but he found himself sobbing on his knees. The officers backed off, making space. John Griffin and Tom exchanged guilt ridden expressions as they saw his rage pass into grief and then melt into sorrow.

CHAPTER ELEVEN

———— ◆◇◆ ————

Through the dark sleet of rain outside, Casey stretched his mind far away from the hospital window. Wind shook the trees in the courtyard, swaying the branches like wild brush strokes across the sky. Two orderlies entered almost soundless. They covered his mother with a white sheet and pulled her towards her ashes. Casey craned his head away from the window and watched her drift away on a bed of clouds. The sound of silence was deafening. The sound of silence left Casey alone in a sea of undoing, lost on tides of despair, that he tried to navigate, tried to float upon boards of numbness. But the blindness sunk in and he with it.

CHAPTER TWELVE

◆ ◇ ◆

"In your mercy, turn the darkness of death into the dawn of new life, and the sorrow of parting into the joy of heaven..."

Father O'Brian recited his final prayer, two urns stood beside one another.

Casey sat blankly as the priest's words offered little solace.

The ceremony ended and Father O'Brian approached Casey in consolation. Casey stood to meet him, shaking his hand. His eyes were distant. The world was a distant place. So far, the constant distraction of his mother's will, the funeral and all the legal matters had postponed his grieving. But, today marked the end of that. Casey stood tall as people offered their condolences, he met their eyes as best he could and shook their hands. Eventually, he found himself alone.

The rain had stopped, but clouds still veiled the sky in grey. The sea roared torrents of power, unrelenting, waves crashed against the rocky stretch, where Casey stood, at the apex of its reach. A tiny figure amidst the vast, unsettled sea.

Casey tipped his mother's ashes first for the ocean to swallow and carry. For her spirit to ride the waves and travel the tides pulled by the moon. He placed the empty urn down on the rocks, then picked up his brother. It took him a lot more to lift the lid. It took Casey a lot longer to let Walter go. His heart shook and tore in his chest like the waves crashing around him.

With the weight of the world's oceans on his heart, he let his brother's ashes spill. The wind carried them far away into the horizon. Or at least that's what Casey saw.

He saw his brother travelling to the ends of the earth.

He saw his brother come to rest with the wind and sea.

He saw his brother and mother together once again.

Casey dropped to his knees, as his grief overcame him. His emotions and the ocean became a blur. When his emotions crashed, so did the waves. There were no words, no single thought. Casey's mind was lost in the primordial swell of emotions, a mirror of the natural world around him.

He begged the ocean to take him too, screamed for it, screamed from that wordless place. The ocean burst and sprayed around him, but she did not pull him in. Eventually it settled and the sky began to clear, light cut through the clouds in spotlights over the vast ocean and finally, Casey ceased his song to the sea.

~

Birds sung in the late afternoon, and families walked hand in hand making banter. In the front lawn of the Treggar home was a fresh *For Sale* sign. Casey loaded the last few items into his truck. The entire day memories of his childhood in this house had replayed themselves continuously.

Casey stepped onto the front porch and turned to look at the empty house, through the open door. He had spent his whole life here. The moments of hide and seek with Walter, hiding in closets, washing machines and other obscure places. Playing catch, wrestling in the yard. Their mom having to intervene when the wrestling became too wild and competitive. He remembered the prayers before dinner, and the stories before bed. They streamed through his mind one after another until tears encased his eyes in crystal.

As a final goodbye, Casey lay his palm on the outer wall of the house. Silently, he thanked her for keeping them safe, for allowing so many moments to happen. And when Casey shut the door, so too were the memories sealed behind.

He turned away with a sigh and noticed Julia standing at the end of the driveway. She smiled a heavy smile. One that recognized all the pain they had been through, one that was happy to see him, one full of love. Casey couldn't hide the surprise he felt, nor the strange mix of emotions that rose, joy to heartbreak…

"Hey."

"Hey." Casey replied.

Julia pulled Casey into her eyes. He could show her everything, the pain, the grief. All of it. The silence between them was tangible and electric. There was a long pause before Julia broke the silence.

"So, where are you gonna go?"

"I have no idea." He smiled.

"Well, it looks like for the first time, you are doing what *you* want."

"Yeah… It's a change."

She nodded, smiling out of love for him, and yet tears still formed in her eyes.

"I'm sorry Casey. — We're both sorry."

Casey nodded, he gently pulled her in for a hug. One that was to console and nothing more. After a few breaths Julia drew back and handed Casey a familiar bag. It was the gift he had given her.

"I wanted to get this back to you. It was your moms. I can't…"

Casey understood. "Thank you."

Julia took one final look at him and smiled before turning and leaving back towards her husband and son who awaited in their car. John Griffin noticed Casey's eyes on him and gave him a sincere nod of apology. Casey nodded back.

That was it.

He watched as they drove off.

When they disappeared, he made his way over to his truck and patted her on the back.

"Just you and me now."

Almost every step was a sigh, but it helped him to breathe, to cope with everything. He reversed out of the driveway and pulled onto the road, sparing one last look at the only place he had called home. Then, with a genuine smile he drove off, leaving it all behind.

As Casey wove through the town, he could see his memories overlaid across the town's streets and monuments, such as the barber shop, where Casey happened to spot two boys leaving with their father, both sporting identical five-dollar haircuts. Casey smiled in reflection.

He saw himself as a child, as a teenager, as a grown man in every spot he drove past. The Talisman hotel, the pier and main street. Every corner of this town, he knew like the back of his hand. And now for the first time in his life he was leaving, a lifetime in a single second gone with the wind.

He opened his windows as he got on the long stretch of road that left Westport. The wind tossed Casey's hair wildly and so easily the open road took him.

Weightless and still tethered to the earth, for the first time in his life, Casey was unbound with the unknown before him.

'UNSPOKEN'
WRITER'S BIOGRAPHY

Michael Adante is a writer and filmmaker whose work has spanned feature films, advertising and television production.

Adante produced & directed the feature film 'THE LINE' in 2007 and completed his second feature production 'VANISHED' in 2011, which was released in a number of territories globally; Australia, Europe, Asia & North America.

Adante is an avid reader and passionate about story and how it engages, entertains and evolves humanity. UNSPOKEN marks his first novel.

He currently resides in Brisbane, Australia & West Hollywood, California with wife and daughter.